"Do you need any help getting ready for bed?"

"Are you offering to help me undress?" Bobby asked teasingly. "Guess it won't be much different from when we were living together, right?"

She gave him a sharp look, and he smiled at her. "What do you remember of that time?" she asked.

"It's hard to say. I remember kissing you, and enjoying it immensely. I'm sure if I really put my mind to it, I'll be able to remember what it was like to make love to you…unless you want to help me refresh my memory," he couldn't resist adding.

"You'd have a tough time recalling anything like that," she replied tartly, "because we never slept together…."

"Ah, well, that explains why I don't remember." But that didn't stop him from hoping it would happen now that Casey had come back into his life….

❧ ❧ ❧ ❧ ❧

Attention all Annette Broadrick fans, don't miss *Unforgettable Bride*, a charming spin-off from her popular DAUGHTERS OF TEXAS series.

Dear Reader,

Unforgettable Bride, by bestselling author Annette Broadrick, is May's VIRGIN BRIDES selection, *and* the much-requested spin-off to her DAUGHTERS OF TEXAS series. Rough, gruff rodeo star Bobby Metcalf agreed to a quickie marriage—sans honeymoon!—with virginal Casey Carmichael. But four years later, he's still a married man—one intent on being a husband to Casey in every sense....

Fabulous author Arlene James offers the month's FABULOUS FATHERS title, *Falling for a Father of Four.* Orren Ellis was a single dad to a brood of four, so hiring sweet Mattie Kincaid seemed the perfect solution. Until he found himself falling for this woman he could never have.... Stella Bagwell introduces the next generation of her bestselling TWINS ON THE DOORSTEP series. In *The Rancher's Blessed Event,* an ornery bronc rider must open his heart both to the woman who'd betrayed him...and her child yet to be born.

Who can resist a sexy, stubborn cowboy—particularly when he's your husband? Well, Taylor Cassidy tries in Anne Ha's *Long, Tall Temporary Husband.* But will she succeed? And Sharon De Vita's irresistible trio, LULLABIES AND LOVE, continues with *Baby with a Badge,* where a bachelor cop finds a baby in his patrol car...and himself in desperate need of a woman's touch! Finally, new author C.J. Hill makes her commanding debut with a title that sums it up best: *Baby Dreams and Wedding Schemes.*

Romance has everything you need from new beginnings to tried-and-true favorites. Enjoy each and every novel this month, and every month!

Warm Regards!

Joan Marlow Golan

Joan Marlow Golan
Senior Editor, Silhouette Romance

VIRGIN BRIDES

Annette Broadrick

UNFORGETTABLE BRIDE

Silhouette
R O M A N C E™
Published by Silhouette Books
America's Publisher of Contemporary Romance

This one's for you, Ryan

 SILHOUETTE BOOKS

ISBN 0-373-19294-0

UNFORGETTABLE BRIDE

Printed in U.S.A.

ANNETTE BROADRICK

Since 1984, when her first book was published, Annette has shared her view of life and love with readers all over the world. In addition to being nominated by *Romantic Times* as one of the Best New Authors of that year, she has won the *Romantic Times'* Reviewers' Choice Award for Best in its Series, the *Romantic Times'* WISH award, and the *Romantic Times'* Lifetime Achievement Awards for Series Romance and Series Romantic Fantasy.

Dear Reader,

There's just something about weddings and brides that seems to appeal. It's a time of hope and love and anticipation and a tingling anxiety that all will be well.

No one who has ever been a bride can forget that day in her life. Regardless of what happens later in her marriage, her wedding day is a memorable experience.

And so it should be.

One of my favorite stories has to do with seeing how two almost strangers can work out their differences and create a bond that cannot be broken. Whenever someone mentions brides to me, I think of impetuous, impulsive young women who somehow want to take charge of their lives and still have that one particular person in their life who makes them feel loved and needed and wanted.

Unforgettable Bride is one of those stories. I found while writing this particular book that both of my characters were unforgettable—individuals who lingered in my memory long after I finished their story.

I hope that they linger in yours, as well.

Annette Broadrick

Chapter One

Casey Carmichael pushed on the heavy door of the local saloon, forcing it open, and stepped inside, leaving the gloom of the night behind her. The unfamiliar scent of cigarette smoke swirled around her, causing her eyes to burn and her throat to tingle. She stifled a cough in an effort to remain unnoticed while she peered through the blue haze.

He had to be here somewhere in this noisy room— he just had to be. She'd already found out that he hadn't left town, even though he'd lost the rodeo events he'd entered this week. If she hadn't heard one of the stable hands mention his name earlier today and that this particular Texas panhandle saloon was his hangout whenever he was in town, perhaps she would never have gotten the idea to seek him out. Once the idea struck her, however, she could think of nothing else.

She was desperate, although she didn't want him to know that. Somehow she had to convince him that what she proposed would benefit both of them. In her case, she had nothing to lose. In his case, she hoped she could make the offer sound appealing enough that he would at least consider her suggestion.

The door made a groaning, whooshing sound as it closed behind her, signaling to the occupants of the place that someone had entered the portals of their Friday night palace. Perhaps palace didn't quite describe the place, Casey thought, glancing around the long, narrow room. The scarred, wide-planked floors and plaster walls had long ago lost any paint that might have helped them to gleam in the dim light.

Casey adjusted her Stetson, pulling it low over her eyes. Her long braid was concealed inside the hat. In the hope of at least temporarily disguising her gender, she'd worn her oldest jeans and a battered denim jacket several sizes too large for her, which she'd found in the horse barn.

From the stares she was getting, she wasn't certain her disguise was working. Then again, maybe it was customary for the inhabitants of the bar to examine each new arrival. Since this was the first time she'd ever been in such a place, the customary social etiquette for this particular situation was a mystery to her.

Casey straightened her shoulders and deliberately scanned the room with a bored expression. Soon enough, faces turned away and conversations resumed. Casey gave a silent prayer of thanks before searching the room to locate the man she'd risked her reputation and her future to find.

She knew him only by his notoriety, plus a glimpse of a snapshot taken of him after one of his bull-riding events a few years back. Given the poor lighting and the pervasive blue haze of the room, Casey wasn't at all certain she'd recognize him tonight. She could only hope.

The door suddenly swung open behind her, almost knocking her into a table. She hastily stepped farther into the room. A raucous group of celebrating cowboys pushed through the door, surrounding her while they boisterously discussed the rodeo.

Quickly she scanned each face, but none looked familiar. Dawdling in front of the door wasn't getting her anywhere, she realized with a mental nudge. In as casual a manner as she could muster, Casey sauntered alongside the bar that stretched to the back of the room, her gaze darting between the row of booths on one side and the occupied barstools on the other. No one fit the description of the man she desperately sought. She would not panic.

Casey tried to recall all that she had heard about the man. He was a loner, for one thing. At least when he lost, as he had today. So he would probably be alone.

No sooner had the thought occurred to her, than Casey spotted a shadowy figure in the last booth. Alone. He had successfully discouraged others from joining him by propping his feet, encased in well-worn boots and crossed at the ankles, on the bench seat across from him.

This could very well be the man she'd been searching for. Casey swallowed hard and willed her knees not to quiver now that she had gotten this far in her quest.

She paused beside the man and waited for him to glance up at her.

He ignored her presence, his attention steadfastly fixed on the longneck bottle of beer in front of him. The brim of his hat concealed all but the lower third of his face. All she could see of the man was a well-shaped jawline, but there was something about him—his attitude, maybe?—that caused her to think she'd found the right man.

After clearing her throat, Casey asked, "Are you Bobby Metcalf?"

The man didn't respond or move for several long seconds. Casey wondered if he'd even heard her over the noise in the place, until he finally replied without glancing up.

"Who wants to know?" His gruff voice sounded rusty.

She sat down on the edge of the seat across from him in an effort to see his face. From this angle, she was able to see high cheekbones, shadowed eyes and a nose that had been broken more than once.

"My name is Casey Carmichael. If you're Bobby Metcalf, I need to speak to you."

"What about?"

Although she'd spent the time driving into town rehearsing what she would say to him when she found him, now that she was here, her mind had gone blank. Casey leaned her arms on the table and peered beneath the brim of his hat in an effort to see his eyes. "*Are you Bobby?*"

"Maybe," he drawled. "Who the hell are you, and what do you want?"

"Some degree of politeness would do for starters," she snapped back before she could stop herself. She almost groaned out loud. This was not going as she had hoped it would.

He lifted his gaze from the bottle in front of him, pinning her to her seat with his cold stare. "You're the one who came in here lookin' for me, sugar. I'm just sittin' back here mindin' my own business, leavin' everybody else alone. You might try it sometime.''

Casey could feel herself flushing. She straightened her spine and inched farther back on the bench seat. ''Look,'' she said quietly, ''I really need your help or I wouldn't be here. A friend once told me about you, and I—''

''What friend is that?''

''Dolores Bennett. DeeDee and I—''

''Never heard of her,'' he said dismissively and picked up the bottle in front of him, draining the contents. He set the empty bottle down with one hand and signaled the waitress for another drink with the other one.

The waitress came over, cleared away the empty bottle and looked at Casey. ''What can I getcha?''

Casey ordered a cola, then waited until the waitress turned away before saying, ''DeeDee's brother used to follow the circuit. He—''

''You talking about Bulldog Bennett?'' he asked with a more pronounced drawl, the first sign of amusement— or any other kind of emotion—she'd heard in his voice.

''Uh, his name is Brad. I don't know—''

''Same guy. So you know Bulldog, do you?''

''Not well. His sister and I went through school together. Their family has a ranch near Cielo.''

The waitress returned with their drinks. The man across from Casey slid some money she hadn't noticed on the table toward the waitress and murmured, ''Keep the change.''

The waitress flashed him a wide smile. ''Thanks, Bobby,'' she said, smoothly pocketing the money before turning away.

At least Casey now knew she was talking to the right person.

There was no way to gracefully explain why she was there, so Casey plunged into the conversation with what she considered to be the most relevant piece of information that she needed to impart.

"I'm supposed to get married next Saturday," she said in a rush. She hadn't meant to blurt it out quite so abruptly, but then, none of her training in manners had ever envisioned her present situation.

"Congratulations," he replied, turning the bottle up for a long swallow without giving her another glance.

Now came the tough part. "The thing is, I can't go through with it."

He lowered the bottle and looked at her quizzically. "Aren't you telling the wrong person here, sugar? It seems to me that the guy you're supposed to be marrying would appreciate being the first to hear that particular piece of news."

DeeDee hadn't bothered to mention just how sarcastic Bobby Metcalf could be. Then again, Casey wasn't certain how well DeeDee knew Bobby, either. Most of her stories about him had come from her brother. Casey could only hope that they hadn't been exaggerated, and that he was as unconventional as his reputation made him out to be.

"Look, I know I'm not making much sense right now. But when DeeDee told me about you, she said that her brother—" Her voice faded to nothing and she cleared her throat, unable to finish what she'd been going to say because Bobby had stiffened, dropped his feet and straightened in his seat. For the first time, Casey became fully aware of just how intimidating this man could be.

She grabbed her drink and took a hasty swallow, almost choking in her hurry.

"Exactly what did Bulldog say about me?" His voice was even lower than it had been before.

"Well, he…er…well, DeeDee mentioned that…"

"Yes?"

In a rush, she said, "That you once ran off to Vegas and married someone you barely knew."

The noise he made was a mixture of disgust and amusement. "That was a long time ago, sugar, when I was young and stupid. Hopefully I've gotten a little smarter over the years." He eyed his drink thoughtfully before adding, "Then again, there was lots of room for improvement back then." He glanced up at her again. "Why does that old news interest you?"

She cleared her throat once again and said, "What would I have to offer you to get you to marry *me?*"

Whatever she'd expected from Bobby Metcalf when she'd tried to imagine this conversation, she'd never once thought he'd laugh in her face. However, that was exactly what he did, embarrassing her even more.

What had she expected, anyway? They were complete strangers, after all. There was no reason for him to take her seriously. Somehow, she would have to convince him that she'd never been more serious in her life. She just wished she felt more adequate for the job at the moment.

"Now let me get this straight," he finally said, dangling the bottle between his thumb and forefinger. "You've got a wedding all planned in a week's time. Now you're asking someone you don't know to marry you instead? Wouldn't it be simpler just to call off the weddin', sugar?"

If she hadn't already exhausted every other plan she could think of, she would have gotten up and walked out right then and there. Instead, she took another sip of her cola while she reviewed her alternatives. Convincing a stranger to marry her was by far her best option at this point. The trick would be to present her reasons in a calm, rational manner so that he would help her out.

After a lengthy pause she said, "Please let me explain so that you'll understand my dilemma," she began, pleased with her matter-of-fact tone. "I've been engaged to Steve Whitcomb for almost a year. I know how foolish this must sound to you, but I only recently realized that the only reason I agreed to marry Steve in the first place was to please my father." Casey studied the ice cubes in her glass, hating to put into words feelings that had been apparent to her most of her life. She forced herself to meet the steady gaze across from her and said in a low voice, "Steve is everything my dad always wanted in a son, you see. I've always been aware of what a disappointment I was." With a tiny shrug she said, "Who knows? Maybe I thought that if I married someone my dad liked I would win his approval a little easier. Besides, I really thought I was in love with Steve back then. He treated me as though I was someone special, as though I really mattered and was important to him." She glanced away and gave her head a quick shake. "I actually believed him when he said he'd been waiting all his life for me." She swallowed, remembering how easy she'd been to convince and how humiliated she'd been when she found out the truth about the man. "I found out quite by accident a few weeks ago that he's been involved with another woman during our entire engagement. He doesn't love me. He never loved me. He's a lying, cheating hypocrite who—''

''Whoa now, sugar,'' Bobby interjected. ''I wasn't asking for a list of your intended's qualifications in the marriage market. Look, if you don't want to marry him, why don't you just call the thing off?''

''You think I haven't tried? When I confronted Steve he laughed in my face and suggested that I talk to my father about my feelings. Unfortunately my father is convinced I'm too young to know my own mind about the kind of man I need to marry. Since he feels as though he handpicked the man who will someday take over his so-called empire, I'm supposed to accept the fact that I'm just going through the usual prewedding bridal jitters. According to my dad, I'm supposed to overlook Steve's girlfriend. In fact, my dad was more upset that I had found out about her than he was that she existed in Steve's life. He was actually muttering to me about how a man needed to learn discretion and that he'd have to talk to Steve about that!''

''And what does your mother have to say about it?''

''I have no idea. She left my father when I was eight years old. I've never heard from her since. If he treated her the way he treats me, it's no wonder she left. According to my father, women weren't born with a brain or any reasoning power. Therefore we need men to do all our thinking for us.''

Bobby took another long drink from his bottle. When he set it on the table he stared into her face as though trying to place her in his memory. ''What did you say your name is?''

''Casey Carmichael.''

As though she had confirmed something for him he nodded, then picked up the beer bottle again. This time he drained it. "Graham Carmichael's daughter, huh? Looks like you inherited your old man's nerve, asking a stranger to marry you like this. What are you tryin' to do here, cook up some little ol' scandal to get your powerful daddy to pay more attention to you?"

She didn't say anything for fear that she would start screaming at him. Were all men as obnoxious as the ones she'd had the misfortune of being around, or had she just managed to attract a group of them into her life as some sort of heavenly punishment? Maybe this guy wasn't the one to help her after all. Maybe she was being a complete idiot about this. Nobody, not even her wealthy, power-hungry papa, could actually force her into marrying a man she intensely disliked.

So maybe Bobby Metcalf was doing her a real favor here. She wouldn't want to be married, even though it would only be a legal formality, to someone this hateful.

Slowly she nodded her head. "Yeah, I guess you're right. I'm just starved for attention, that's all. Well, Mr. Metcalf, I'm very sorry to have bothered you. Why don't you continue to sit there and drink yourself senseless while I just get on with my life."

She slid across the bench seat only to discover that sometime during their friendly little chat Bobby had propped one of his booted feet back on the seat beside her, this time blocking her exit.

"How old are you, little girl?"

"What possible difference does it make? If you'll kindly move your foot, I'll get out of here."

"Indulge me a little, okay? Sorry if I riled you, but you've gotta admit that what you're asking is pretty bizarre. So what you're saying is, because Bulldog told you that old story about me, you thought I'd be willing to run off and marry you, too?"

She gritted her teeth. "What I want is my freedom—from Steve, from my father, from my entire way of life. I thought if I entered into a business arrangement with someone who would be willing to help me, we'd both get what we want."

"Exactly what is it you think I want that you can give me?" he asked, intrigued despite himself.

"I heard that you've been saving your money to buy a place of your own."

"So?"

"I have money in a trust fund that will come to me once I'm married. I'm willing to split the money with you."

"How old did you say you were?"

"I didn't say. For your information I'm eighteen years old."

"That old, huh? Kinda explains a lot of things. First of all, it's not smart to go offering strangers your money. There's no telling who might be stupid enough to take you up on it. Secondly, bribing a fellow to help you out in a bind isn't very complimentary on your part. And third, what in the hell were you thinking of, planning to get married so young? Why would your dad encourage such a thing, anyway?"

"Steve was the one who wanted to marry as soon as I was finished with high school. I thought I'd be going on to college, despite getting married. I really thought Steve understood how much I wanted to continue my education and would agree to it. I've wanted to be a veterinarian as far back as I can remember. That's all I've talked about for years. Now I realize that neither Steve nor my dad see any point in my going on to school and that Steve was just indulging me my dreams until after we were actually married."

"How old is this Steve character?"

"I don't know. Somewhere over thirty. Thirty-two, I think."

"That ancient, is he? I hate to bust your bubble, sugar, but I'm no spring chicken, either. I'm looking real hard at that big three-oh, myself."

"I don't care how old you are. I was counting on the fact that once I proved to my father and to Steve that I was married to someone else and that there was no way I would ever marry Steve, then I figured you and I would have our marriage annulled and go our separate ways. When DeeDee told me about you, you seemed to be a perfect candidate." Her tone of voice indicated that she had since reconsidered his suitability.

Bobby sighed. "My one claim to fame—impulsively marrying a stranger in Vegas. I guess that story will dog my steps for the rest of my days."

"I wouldn't say it was your *one* claim. You're much too modest. You're also known as a world champion bull rider, calf-roper and—"

"Don't remind me. Every morning when I crawl out of bed my body sends all kinds of signals about my foolish and misspent past."

She eyed him with a hint of curiosity. "Are you considering taking me up on my offer?"

He smiled and shook his head. "Look, sugar, you've been downright entertaining, and I can't say that I haven't enjoyed your story, but I want no part in any of your plans. Have you ever considered that your papa may be right? That this is just prewedding jitters? It happens, you know. This Steve guy probably isn't all that bad. What gave you the idea he's seeing somebody else?"

"You mean besides the two-year-old he fathered with

this woman? Or that he's been laughing with all his friends about the fact he's engaged to me, thinking I wouldn't find out that I've become a joke to him? Or maybe—"

"Never mind, I get the picture. And your father doesn't care about any of that?"

"He thinks I'm too sensitive. He said if I'm half the woman he thinks I am, I'll be able to keep Steve's interest at home." Her voice registered her disgust.

"I don't know anything about that. All I know is that I'm not willing to help you get back at your daddy and his handpicked stud." He slid out of his seat and stood. Looking down at her, he said, "I need to get some sleep. I'm heading out early in the morning. I suggest you get on back home before somebody misses you. We'll just pretend we never had this conversation, okay?"

Casey also stood and immediately turned away, fighting the tears that would instantly betray her to this hateful, hateful man. She strode toward the door without looking around. She didn't wait to see if Bobby was behind her when she jerked open the door and stepped outside the saloon onto the graveled parking lot.

She blinked back the tears from her eyes and looked around the crowded lot. There were cars and trucks pulling in and leaving, and a great deal of loud talking and laughing. Casey was out of her element, and she knew it. She'd been stupid to even try this. She didn't need Bobby Metcalf in order not to get married. She'd go back home tonight, but tomorrow she'd manage a way to leave again, this time with some of her things. She'd go to Vegas by herself and hide out for a few days. After that, she might even continue west and visit California. No one was going to force her into a marriage she didn't want.

Casey lifted her chin. She was not going to play victim. Once Steve and her father saw that she had no intention of being present at any wedding they might have set up, they'd get the idea she couldn't be pushed around.

She threaded her way through the crowded parking lot to where she'd left her car, which had been a high school graduation present a few weeks ago. She'd been so innocent of all the strings attached to any gift her father gave her back then. At the time she had actually felt the car was a sign that he loved her. She felt as though she'd aged a dozen years since then. Talk about some wishful thinking. She'd spent most of her life in serious denial. But no more. She was going to face facts, face reality and take charge of her life.

Starting now.

She spotted her car, and only then did she realize that her little roadster had drawn the attention of four men who were standing around it, talking, laughing and drinking from flasks. She was sick and tired of the entire male population at the moment. Casey reached into her coat pocket and grabbed her keys, gripping them tightly in her fist, then continued toward her car.

"Hey, kid," one of the men called to her, "this your car? Or does it belong to your daddy?"

They all laughed at his stupid attempt at humor.

"It's mine," she replied in a flat tone from several yards away, pushing the security button on the key chain, causing the lights to flash a welcome as the doors unlocked.

The group's mood immediately changed and she realized what she'd just done. Her disguise had worked in the ill-lighted parking lot until she spoke.

"Well, now, honey-bunch, how's about you and me takin' a little ride in your pretty toy car?" the apparent leader of the group asked. "I might even be talked into showing you some fancy riding of my own."

His friends laughed and waited to see what she would say.

At the moment, she was too angry at the world in general and men in particular to be scared. So she ignored him and continued toward the car.

The loudmouthed one stepped over in front of her, blocking her path. "Did you hear me, honey? Tonight could be your lucky night."

She looked up at him and said, "No, thanks, bubba. I think I'll pass." She stepped around him, and reached for the door handle.

Just as the door swung open the guy grabbed her by the arm and said, "Hey now, don't be that way."

Casey didn't resist the tug on her arm, allowing the momentum to build as her body swung around. She gave a lightning-quick kick, catching him in a very vulnerable spot between the legs while at the same time letting her fist, with keys protruding from between her fingers, connect rather forcefully with his chin.

Then, for some unknown reason, World War III seemed to break out around her. All right, so maybe she shouldn't have done it, she decided judiciously as his friends let out a roar that almost matched their friend who was currently writhing on the ground, using language that should never be spoken around a lady.

Someone else grabbed her, yelling something she couldn't understand, this time knocking off her hat, which—for some reason or another—became the last straw in a day of losing arguments with every male she'd encountered.

She struck back, even as she heard a quiet voice from somewhere beyond the group crowding around her say, "Let her go."

Despite the moaning and yelling that seemed to be on all sides of her, Casey recognized Bobby's voice before she had a chance to look around.

Didn't these guys know anything about fighting? Just because she was shorter and weighed less was no reason for them to underestimate her. The one gripping her shoulder immediately let go as soon as her knee came into contact with his oh-so-tender anatomy, while a third man stepped back to face Bobby.

"Butt out, mister. This is none of your business."

The next man had just reached for her when his knees buckled beneath him and she saw that Bobby was standing there rubbing his knuckles. "Get in the car!" he yelled at her, which she did, fumbling to find the right key. Suddenly he was there in the doorway beside her, lifting her into the other seat as though she weighed no more than a rag doll and sliding behind the wheel, himself. Gunning the engine, he spun the car out of the parking lot, leaving several angry men yelling and running after them, shaking their fists.

"I don't know how in the hell you managed to stay alive for eighteen whole years if you're in the habit of pulling stupid stunts like that," he growled, watching the rearview mirror while they sped down the road. "Do you have some kind of death wish, or something?"

"I was angry," she replied defensively. "I'm fed up with being treated like a blasted ornament on a man's arm, or a moron who can't make decisions for herself. I'm tired of dealing with macho men who think just because they're bigger and stronger they can do anything they want, while I'm supposed to be flattered by their attention. What I'm really angry about is that I'm only eighteen years old. At twenty-five I get my inheritance, married or not. You can tell my grandfather was from another century. He probably decided that if I couldn't find a man willing to marry me by that age, then there wasn't a man anywhere who would want me.''

Bobby drove for a while in silence, mulling over various ways he might be able to reach this agitated, obviously distressed woman. Finally he said, ''I don't think getting married is the answer, Casey.''

''Actually, neither do I,'' she instantly replied, surprising him. ''Unless, of course,'' she went on, ''it's a marriage that is clearly understood by both parties. All I wanted from you was your signature on a marriage license. That piece of paper will give me the freedom I need from my dad's plotting and planning with Steve, and it will give me access to the money that was left to me, so that I can go to school. I want nothing from you but your name in exchange for half my inheritance. I can't see why you or anyone else would pass up a deal like that, but then it's been recently proved to me rather obviously that I know absolutely nothing about men.''

''You don't know much about *me* is the point I've been trying to make with you this evening,'' Bobby pointed out with exasperation. ''I could be a serial killer for all you know. Although, I have to admit from what I saw back there you may be more capable of looking after yourself than I thought, even though you're not too good at calculating odds.''

She ignored his last statement. Instead she addressed

the first. "Brad knows you. DeeDee says he's known you for several years, ever since you went on the circuit. Even though he didn't know why DeeDee and I were asking so many questions about you, he made it clear you could be trusted to keep your word."

She could barely see his face in the dim light from the dash of the car, but she could have sworn he flinched at her last remark.

"I learned a little too late about keeping my word, but Brad's right. I finally discovered how important a person's word is."

"It doesn't matter now, anyway. You were right. It was a stupid idea, but at least I managed to get away from the house. I managed to convince my dad that I'm resigned to getting married to Steve. Otherwise, he wouldn't have allowed me to leave. The more I think about it, the more I've decided not to risk going back." Which meant, she thought to herself, that she would have to figure a way to buy some clothes to wear for the next few weeks.

"So where were you planning to go, before you attracted your admiring audience back there?"

"I hope you're not trying to blame what happened back there on me!" she said, hoping to distract him from his question. She had a hunch he wouldn't be any more impressed with her new plan than he was with her original one. "That guy had no business touching me."

"You're absolutely right. He didn't. But didn't you notice that your admirer had three rather protective friends that might take offense at your rejection of him?"

"I wasn't thinking about them."

"Obviously."

"Where are we going?" she asked, glancing around at the swiftly moving landscape sliding by.

"Anywhere away from this part of town until those guys cool off. Did you know any of them?"

"Of course not! I never saw them before in my life."

"Well, they're certainly going to remember you and this little red car of yours."

She slid down in her seat. "At the moment, those guys are the least of my worries."

When he finally slowed and turned she realized that he was pulling into a truck stop. "Why are we stopping?"

He glanced around at her in irritation. "Why? Because I doubt that your car has been weaned to go on fumes, that's why. The gas gauge is buried beneath the Empty mark."

"Oh."

"My God, woman. You really need a keeper, don't you? You hadn't noticed how much gas was left in the car?"

"My mind was on other things."

"Like trying to find some idiot to marry you."

"I've given up on that."

"I'm glad to hear it. So what are you going to do if you don't go back home tonight?"

"What difference does it make to you?"

"Indulge me, okay? There's just something about the way your mind works that makes me a little nervous, that's all. Granted, I happen to agree that you shouldn't have to marry someone you don't want to. I just think you're being a little dramatic about all of this, that's all. If you aren't going home, then where are you going? To your friend's place? Brad's sister?"

"No. That's the first place my dad would look for

me." She sighed, knowing that her newest plan wasn't going to be favorably received by this man, either. "I'm going to Vegas by myself, stay there a few days, then maybe drive to California. I've always wanted to visit Los Angeles. My father will never think to look for me out of the state."

He pulled up in front of the pumps and got out before he burst into outraged speech at this latest sign of her complete idiocy.

She jumped out on the other side and said, "Here's my card."

He looked at the pumps that gave an option to use a credit card, then he looked down at her card, shaking his head at the whole situation. "This belongs to your father, right?"

She frowned. "Yes. Why?"

"You don't mind using his money even while you intend to run away from him, is that it? That's your idea of defying him?"

"Look, I know what you're thinking, that I'm some spoiled rich girl who has had everything she ever wanted. Everything but what I wanted most, to live my own life. My dad wouldn't let me work, so I insisted on helping out in the stables to justify the money he gave me. Believe me, I've earned every penny of it."

"Have you thought about the fact that if you use your car and card, your father can find you by reporting you as missing to the police?"

"He wouldn't do that."

"Hell, I would, if you belonged to me. The way your mind works, I'd be afraid you'd be out kickboxing drug smugglers or escaped convicts."

"All right, so I won't use my card. I've got cash. I'll

pay cash until I run out. I can always get more from an ATM—''

"Which your father could have checked easily enough, as well. Let's face it, you're in way over your head here.''

She crossed her arms. "I'm not going back home.''

He crossed his arms, mimicking her stubborn stance. "You don't have the sense God gave a goose, girl! Don't you have any idea how dangerous it is for a woman to travel alone? Especially to Vegas! And if you manage by some miracle to survive being mugged or raped there, you intend to visit Los Angeles?'' He threw up his hands in complete disgust, then turned away. He went inside the truck stop, handed the cashier a twenty-dollar bill, then returned to the car and started the pump.

Casey had turned away and was staring out into the night.

He looked over at her, shaking his head. She was much too attractive to think she wasn't going to be noticed and remembered, although he had to admit that she'd camouflaged herself fairly well tonight. She was tall and slender and in that getup she might have passed for a boy as long as she wore her hat. Now that her reddish-brown hair hung in a thick braid down her back, he wondered how anyone could mistake her delicate femininity for a male, regardless of how young.

He'd seen her face for the first time when she'd been standing there under the bright lights of the truck stop arguing with him about the gasoline. He'd been astonished at how young and vulnerable she'd looked. She walked with a confident stride, her voice was cool and very assured, but her face, and especially her clear, wide-set, whiskey-colored eyes, gave her away.

She was running scared. In that mood, there was no telling what damn-fool thing she'd do next.

The gasoline cut off with an audible snap. Bobby recapped the tank, hung up the hose and walked inside to get his change. He intended to have her drop him off back at the tavern to pick up his truck. Hopefully they'd been gone long enough for the crowd outside the place to disperse.

None of this was his business, after all. Just because some harebrained female happened to hear about his checkered past didn't mean that he owed her another thought.

So why was he still thinking about her, wondering about her, fearing for her?

Because he was an idiot, that's why.

When he walked outside he found her sitting behind the steering wheel of the car. He crawled into the passenger's side without speaking.

"You didn't need to pay for my gas."

"I know."

She handed him a twenty-dollar bill and started the car. "I'll take you back to the bar. I assume your car is there." She pulled out onto the highway and headed back toward town.

"My truck."

"Whatever."

They made the trip in silence. When she pulled into the driveway of the place, he pointed out his truck and she pulled up in front of it.

He didn't get out right away. Instead, he sat there staring blindly out the front window of the car. Finally, he turned to her and said, "Look, I don't want your money, but if you really think it will help you out of this mess you're in, I'll go to Vegas and marry you.

I think you're making a mistake, but it bothers me to think about what other ideas you'll try to come up with. I'm not sure how much sleep I'd get wondering what you were doing while you were trying to prove how resourceful you can be.''

She turned and faced him, her eyes wide. ''Do you mean it? Really?''

''Yeah, I think I do. The thing is that I want you to promise me if we do this that you'll go on to school and get your education, and that you won't go around offering strangers half your inheritance every time you want something from them.'' He glanced at her and was dismayed to see that tears were sliding down her cheeks. ''Now what?'' he asked in exasperation. He hated being around crying women!

''Thank you, Bobby. I'll never be able to thank you enough.''

''Well, you got that right. This will definitely add to the notoriety of my reputation. Now let me grab my gear and we'll get this little show on the road. We've got a lot of miles to cover tonight.''

''You mean we should go now?''

''You said yourself that you weren't going back home. As for me, I need to be on my way to Wyoming for a rodeo I've entered. If you need me for your groom, sugar, you'd better grab me while you can.''

Her chuckle sounded a little watery, but he could see she was trying to get ahold of herself. She glanced down at her shirt and jeans. ''I wish I'd thought to bring some extra clothes with me tonight, but I guess it really doesn't matter what I get married in.''

''We can pick up a change of clothes and something to sleep in once we get there. After driving all night I'm going to need some sleep before we head back.

Besides, it will make the whole thing more convincing to your dad and fiancé if we're there overnight.''

"That makes sense," she said, although she was unable to disguise the sudden flush to her cheeks.

He got out of the car and strode to his truck. After grabbing his gear, he relocked it and left it where it was. This time he walked around to the driver's side and opened the door. "This won't be the first time I had to leave my wheels at some bar. It probably won't be the last. The truck should be safe enough here until we get back. I'll drive until I get sleepy, then you can take over. We've got some hard driving to do. Vegas is eight hundred and fifty miles from here.''

Once again she moved into the passenger seat. "How do you know that?''

"Because I travel all over this part of the country. Driving at night will help, pushing the speed limit will also help. But it's going to be mid-morning tomorrow before we get there. You might as well sleep while you can.''

Bobby pulled out of the parking lot, switching on the radio at the same time. He needed the company of some nighttime music while he mentally beat up on himself for thinking he was being some kind of hero by helping this gal out of what sounded like a real messy situation.

As he drove west, he mentally rehearsed the various conversations he intended to have with Mr. Graham Carmichael and Mr. Steve Whitcomb when he finally got around to meeting them, for causing Casey so much pain in her young life. She deserved better, and by damn, he was determined to see that she got better treatment in the future.

Chapter Two

They were somewhere west of Winslow, Arizona, when Casey began to realize that she might have been just a tiny—say a wee bit—impulsive about getting married to someone else rather than face her fiancé and father. As she drove through the star-studded night with absolutely no moon in sight, she'd had a great deal of time to contemplate her impetuous behavior.

Not for the first time since she slid behind the steering wheel of her car, Casey peeked at the man beside her. Not that he had noticed her furtive glances. He slept soundly as though such a trek over most of the southwestern United States was a perfectly normal occurrence to him.

It probably was, but she didn't find the thought particularly comforting. She tried to remember why she'd thought he would be the answer to her problems...because he'd done something this unusual before? Exactly how was that a recommendation? she wondered to herself.

Hadn't he turned her down at first? Now that she thought about it, she couldn't quite remember why he had changed his mind. The thought that came suddenly and very clearly to her was that he had been drinking when he made the decision.

Omigod! What if he didn't remember his decision once he sobered up? What if he had a serious drinking problem? What if once they were married he decided to keep her as his wife, as a slave to him and his appetites. What if—

No! She was being silly. Of course she was.

Casey glanced at him again. There really wasn't anything to see, since he'd propped his Stetson over his face, pushed the seat back as far as it would go and was sound asleep, if the faint snoring noises coming from beneath the hat were any indication.

According to DeeDee—who had sworn it was true— this man had been engaged for several years to his childhood sweetheart. A week before the wedding he'd suddenly—and with no explanation to anyone as far as DeeDee knew—married someone else.

That story had haunted Casey ever since she'd discovered that Steve's reasons for marrying her had nothing to do with any feelings he might have for her. She had been intrigued by the idea that this man had chosen to marry someone he didn't know rather than to go through with a wedding that had been planned for years.

That took some nerve.

However, now that she thought about it, Casey wasn't at all certain that his actions had been particularly admirable. There was a certain cowardice to running away, she was beginning to discover, that made her feel as though she had modeled her behavior on someone with an alarming lack of ethics. In fact, she had bribed him to behave in a similar fashion. Not that he was leaving someone standing at the altar in this particular incidence.

No, she was the one who, at least figuratively, was doing that.

All of the arguments he made while at the saloon now rose up to haunt her and they continued to replay in her mind. Of course, no one was holding a gun to her head. She could turn the car around right now and go back to Texas, back to her father's ranch, back to Steve and all the wedding plans.

She cringed at the thought. *Let's face it. You're a coward,* she thought to herself. *You know this isn't the way to deal with the situation, but you're doing it anyway.*

Once again she nervously glanced at the man beside her. Surely a serial killer wouldn't actually announce ahead of time that he might be a serial killer…and DeeDee said that Brad had known him for years…but what did that really mean? Once they were married, he could do anything, be anything, he could—

"Getting cold feet?"

The low voice coming from beneath the hat next to her after miles of silence caused her to let out a small shriek.

"Oh, for God's sake. Just turn the car around and let's go back," he said, sounding disgusted as he popped the seat back to its upright position and removed the hat. "I'm surprised you lasted this long."

"Don't be silly. I have no intention of going back there until after we're married."

"You do see how asinine the whole idea is, don't you?"

She glanced at him, then hastily looked away. He

didn't look at all sleepy. She wondered if he'd just been pretending to sleep.

"So why didn't you marry the girl you were supposed to?" she asked, suddenly irritated at his sanctimonious attitude. "What had she ever done to you to deserve you suddenly running off and marrying someone else?"

"Ah, so you've heard the whole story, have you? Then I'm really surprised that you came looking for me for this little escapade."

"I thought you'd understand," she muttered half under her breath.

"For your information, I did both of us a favor when I didn't marry Maribeth way back when, but I'm not proud of the way I handled it. I don't think you're going to be very pleased with yourself, either." When she didn't say anything, he added, "It isn't too late to turn back, though."

"Yes, it is," she admitted ruefully. "We're more than halfway there. My dad will already be calling all my friends looking for me."

"Does anyone else know about this scheme of yours?"

"No. I didn't want anyone to be forced to lie for me."

"Noble of you."

"Look, Mr. Metcalf, all of this may seem like a joke to you, but believe me, it's no joke to me. This is my life we're talking about."

"Oh? And how do you think it's going to affect me, Ms. Carmichael? Do you think I really enjoy my particular reputation for being irresponsible and uncaring of other people's feelings? If so, then think again. I thought I was finally living down what I did to Maribeth. She and Chris have made a great life for themselves, much better than anything I could have had with her, which is the only reason I'm able to sleep nights. So now I'm going to have you on my conscience. I don't seem to ever learn, do I?''

She didn't have anything to say to that. Maybe she would regret the way she was handling her present situation. Maybe she was making the biggest mistake of her life. But all she had to do was to remember her last conversation with Steve and she knew without a doubt that she would rather face anything than to be married to that man, even if she couldn't convince her father of that fact.

''Tell me about her,'' she asked, hoping to get her mind off her own situation.

''Who?'' He sounded as though he had no idea who they had just been discussing.

''Your fiancée...Maribeth, didn't you call her? And who is Chris? Is that who she finally married? Did you know him? Do you ever see her? Are you friends?''

''What business is it of yours?''

''None whatsoever. I just thought it would help pass the time if you'd talk to me.''

''Oh, I see. My life history is open for discussion, but not yours.''

''I've already told you all there is to know about me. I don't know anything about you.''

''Oh, I don't know. It sounds like ol' Bulldog managed to hit a few of the highlights.''

''You're really sorry you didn't marry her, aren't you?'' she said. ''Well, that's where we're different. I will never regret not marrying Steve, no matter what else happens.''

''I'm not sorry I didn't marry Maribeth, but I'm sorry

as hell about the way I let her know that I couldn't go through with it. I hurt her badly. Thank God Chris was there for her. I had no idea how he felt about her. The three of us grew up together. He was going to be my best man. When I called and told him I'd gotten married within days before the wedding, he offered to marry her in my place. She accepted. End of story.''

''You didn't stay married long, did you?''

''No.''

''Well, you won't need to stay married long this time, either.''

''That's certainly reassuring. I wouldn't want to damage my reputation any.''

''Are you always so sarcastic?''

''Are you always so naive?''

Neither one of them spoke after that, and eventually Bobby took over driving while Casey fell into a restless, dream-filled sleep.

Casey woke suddenly, aware that something had changed. She blinked open her eyes and looked around. They were sitting in an oversize parking lot of a nationally known discount center. It was the car stopping that had awakened her.

She watched as Bobby opened his door and got out. He stretched and groaned, rubbing his back.

''Why are we stopping here?'' she asked, getting out of the car and looking around.

''You said you needed some clothes. This is as good a place as any, unless you think you won't find your type of designer clothing at a discount store.'' His sarcasm was obvious.

Actually, she'd never thought about buying clothes

here before, but she'd never ever admit it to him. "I don't need much, anyway. This will be fine."

She grabbed her purse and marched away, glad they had stopped. Glancing around her, she realized that they must have reached Las Vegas. The dry, desert air seemed to enfold her. She'd visited here once years ago with her father and recognized the mountainous backdrop along the horizon.

They had made good time, she discovered when she checked her watch. She calculated the two-hour time difference from Texas and realized the sun hadn't been up all that long. Glancing at the automatic doors opening in front of her, she noticed the store was open twenty-four hours a day, which certainly made their shopping easier.

Casey immediately went to the drugstore section and picked up some personal toiletries, including a toothbrush and paste, a hairbrush and some deodorant.

Next she tried the clothing section and was amazed at the selection. Before long she was happily trying on a couple of sundresses and a pair of slacks with various blouses.

When she came out of the dressing room she found Bobby waiting for her with folded arms. "I don't think you need an entire wardrobe, Your Highness. We aren't going to be here long enough for you to wear all of that."

She sighed. "Do you have to be such a grump?"

He dropped his arms to his sides and stared at her with unfeigned disgust. "If you'll remember correctly, I haven't had much sleep. If you're so all-fired determined for us to get married, then I suggest we get on with the details of planning a wedding, if it's all the same to you."

He didn't notice the gray-haired lady immediately behind him whose eyes widened at his irritated tone and
the content of his speech. It was obvious to Casey that
the woman was already drawing her own conclusions
about why he hadn't slept all night and why she was
insisting they get married right away.

Casey could feel herself flushing when the woman
studied them both with a disapproving look before
pushing her cart away. For an insane moment Casey
wanted to rush after her with an explanation, but then
what could she say that would make the situation seem
any better than what the woman was already thinking?

So she contented herself with giving Bobby a glare
and gathering her purchases in the basket she was using.
Without a word she quickly checked out at the front
counter, then went into the rest room to change clothes.

She took her time combing out her hair, then carefully arranged it in a swirl at the nape of her neck. She
decided it made her look older, which was a good thing.
She needed all the help she could get.

Casey wasn't at all certain the dress helped her mature image. It was a cream-colored cotton dress with
tiny straps over the shoulders. In the dressing room it
had looked festive enough to double as a wedding dress,
but now that she looked at it closer, she wondered if it
wasn't more of a vacation style costume.

And what difference did it make, anyway? This
wasn't a real wedding, she reminded herself. If she ever
decided to marry, she was going to take her time to
plan the perfect occasion and the perfect dress. Of
course, she would be marrying the perfect man, as well,
who would be absolutely nothing like Bobby Metcalf
or Steve Whitcomb or even her father.

But all of that would come later. In the meantime,

she would have to get through this day as best she could.

She noticed when they got back in the car that Bobby had shaved and changed into other clothes. His eyes looked bloodshot, which could be caused from all the driving he'd done and the loss of sleep, or the fact that he'd been drinking too much the night before.

She wouldn't say a word to him. Every time they had a verbal exchange she seemed to lose and she was tired of feeling so inept. She was also tired of feeling discounted and ignored by everyone around her.

Well, after today she would be more in control of her own future. She smiled at the thought.

"What evil deeds are you plotting now?" Bobby asked, driving through the morning traffic as though he knew his way around and exactly where he was going.

"What are you talking about? Why would you think I'd be plotting evil deeds?"

"I saw that little smile just now. You're like a cat who just found out where all the cream was stashed."

"I was just thinking about how tired I am of other people having control of my life, that's all. Once I have my inheritance, I'll be independent of everybody. I can hardly wait."

"Unless you spend it all in the first months you have it."

"You don't have to worry about that."

He shrugged. *Why should I care what happens to her, anyway?* he reminded himself. He must have been out of his mind last night agreeing to this nonsense. But he had, so they might as well get the deed done. He was headed to the courthouse to get their license, then they would drop by one of the many places that advertised a quick and easy wedding ceremony. He grinned at the thought.

The first time he was there they'd actually found a judge to marry them at the courthouse. This time he'd decided to give Li'l Miss Carmichael a wedding to remember, just to watch her reaction when she saw what some people would do to manufacture a romantic setting.

He decided a few hours later that it had been well worth the expense just for the look on her face, which he'd managed to have captured on camera by a photographer all too willing to snap pictures of every moment of their treasured journey into the sea of matrimony. He struggled not to laugh out loud at her look of sheer astonishment, not to mention her dismay.

The small chapel had a giant heart at the altar where they would stand as a couple to repeat their vows. Flowers were everywhere, most of them fake.

He had to admit that once she got out of her boyish garb, Ms. Carmichael looked pretty damned good. The full-skirted dress she wore showed off a pair of shapely legs and trim ankles. It was a good thing she'd remembered to buy a pair of sandals at the last minute before leaving the store. Her boots just wouldn't have done the dainty dress any justice, at all.

The fellow marrying them must have noticed that the bride was ignoring the bridegroom with grim determination. In fact, the only words out of her mouth were the ones that she obediently repeated as part of the ceremony. Maybe the guy figured Bobby was better off with a silent bride than a chattering one.

He should be so lucky.

"You may kiss the bride," the man intoned with spurious dignity, reminding Bobby that this was, indeed, a traditional event with carefully set out expectations.

Bobby turned to Casey and quirked an eyebrow. As far as he was concerned, they could certainly skip this part since they had actually participated in a double-ring exchange with symbols that would no doubt turn green on their fingers in a matter of a few hours.

He made the mistake of looking into her eyes and wished he hadn't. She looked bewildered and more than a little lost. She'd done what she set out to do, but it certainly hadn't been a pleasant experience for her. Suddenly he felt bad about what he'd done, which was really making fun of the whole idea of a romantic wedding. She was just a kid, after all, and she was probably recognizing that she had just taken a step into a whole other world.

Which is the only reason why he leaned down to kiss her. He meant to comfort her with a gentle touch of his lips on hers, a gentle reminder that she wasn't alone. However, there wasn't anything gentle about the charge of sheer magnetic energy that seemed to shoot between them when his lips brushed lightly against hers.

She drew in air in a tiny gasp that seemed to echo somewhere deep inside of him. Without a thought, he wrapped his arms around her and snugged her up tight against his chest, continuing the kiss as though he were a dying man in great need of immediate nourishment that only she could provide.

It was only the parson's clearing of his throat that brought Bobby back to where he was and what he was doing. Startled by the sound and the realization that he was kissing the holy bejesus out of a young girl he didn't even know, Bobby dropped his arms and stepped back, only to have to put a hand out to steady Casey, who looked as though she were ready to faint.

"I hope you two lovebirds enjoy your stay here in Vegas." With a knowing grin, the man who had performed the ceremony added, "Even if you don't see much of our fair city this time. It's a great place to visit on your anniversary," he said.

Bobby nodded curtly, took Casey by the elbow and guided her out to her car. She flinched when they walked out into the hot noonday sun. He was automatically reaching for his sunshades when he realized that she probably didn't have any with her. That was another item they could pick up before heading back to Texas.

For the moment, however, all he wanted to do was to find a room somewhere and crash for a few hours. He had the granddaddy of all headaches that a few hours of catch-up sleep should be able to cure. Besides, it was cooler driving the desert area at night.

That was all that was wrong with him, he was sure. That kiss hadn't meant anything at all. It was just that they were both tired, and she was more than a little cranky, and he had just wanted to comfort her a little, just a little, and so maybe he did get carried away with the program. But there was no harm done.

He guided her to the car, opened the passenger door for her, made sure she was tucked inside before he closed the door, then walked around the car to the other side. She was staring down at her hands when he sat down beside her, looking at the ring on the third finger of her left hand.

He'd noticed that she didn't wear rings and he'd guessed at her ring size, but it must have been all right. The fit seemed to be fine. And maybe he had spent a little more on the matching bands than was absolutely necessary, but he wanted her to have something pretty to wear for as long as she needed it.

He started the car and pulled out of the chapel parking lot. Whenever he came to Vegas he generally stayed at a cheap motel on the edge of town, but he didn't think that would be a place to take Casey Carmichael. What the hell, he thought. Might as well go whole hog, here. So he drove down the Strip and pulled into one of the large hotel/casinos. They had put the few things she'd purchased in his bag, so it was no trouble to grab the bag from the back seat and turn the keys to the car over to valet parking.

Bobby kept glancing at Casey, waiting for her to comment or criticize or to do *something,* for God's sake. Instead, she docilely followed his lead. With a brief shake of his head, Bobby grabbed her hand and once again led her to their next destination, this time into the hotel. Registration didn't take long, and in a few minutes they were standing in front of the door of the room he'd paid three months' earnings for.

He opened the door and motioned for her to precede him.

He'd specified two beds and he was pleased to see that they were a good size. At least his feet wouldn't be hanging off the bottom. Maybe it was worth it to bypass the cheap hotels once in a while.

He locked the door behind them. "Pick whatever bed you want. I'm going to shower and crash. I figure after a few hours' sleep, we should be ready to head back sometime this evening, if that's okay with you."

She wandered over to the window and looked out. The view was probably pretty nice from this high up, but Bobby decided he was more interested in a shower than a view.

"Are you okay?" he finally asked, when she didn't answer him.

Without turning around, she murmured, "Yes."

If he didn't have extra-good hearing, he wouldn't have heard that.

With a shrug, he turned away and walked into the bathroom. There was a big tub as well as a glass-enclosed shower. Not bad. Not bad at all.

Within minutes he was under the gushing hot water, whistling as he soaped his body and washed his hair. Maybe he was getting this wedding thing down to a fine science, he decided. He knew he felt a hell of a lot better this time than he had the last time he'd pulled such a stunt.

He only hoped that Casey didn't regret what they had done. If she did, it was too late to do much about it. The deed was done.

Casey Carmichael was now legally Casey Metcalf. He smiled to himself before ducking under the strong spray of water to rinse himself.

Chapter Three

Casey could hear the water running in the other room. Her husband was taking a shower, and from the sounds coming from the area, he was enjoying himself.

She knew beyond a doubt that she was way over her head here. As if that garish, horribly tacky chapel and ceremony hadn't been enough to make her want to run for her life, the kiss at the end of the ceremony had disturbed her much too much.

Her mind kept returning to that kiss, when her world as she knew it disappeared without a trace and she was left in utterly unfamiliar territory.

It was only a kiss, she kept trying to reassure herself. Only a kiss. Then why had it shaken her to the very soul of her being?

Of course she had been kissed before. After all, she and Steve had been engaged for a year. In the past few months she had become uncomfortable around him whenever they were alone because he'd gotten angry a couple of times when he'd urged her to let him make love to her and she had refused. She'd tried to explain that she wanted to wait until after they were married. Later he'd thrown that up to her when she confronted him about the woman he was seeing. He'd told her that the woman wouldn't have been necessary if Casey had been more cooperative, as though it was Casey's fault he'd gotten another woman pregnant.

So of course she'd experienced a great many kisses. Only nothing in her experience had prepared her for the all-consuming rush of desire she'd felt when Bobby Metcalf had wrapped himself around her and shown her what true intimacy felt like!

No wonder people rushed into relationships. If she had responded to Steve that way she wasn't at all certain she could have resisted him. But she didn't want to feel this way about Bobby Metcalf.

From the moment she'd walked into that country bar, Casey had been so absorbed in her own dilemma that she hadn't really thought about Bobby as anything but a possible solution to her troubles. Even later, when she'd gotten so angry at him, she still hadn't thought of him as an attractive male.

She couldn't believe she had been so caught up in her own situation that she'd neglected to notice that Bobby Metcalf was an attractive male animal with a great deal of magnetism.

He looked nothing like Steve, which was a decided plus. Steve was taller and wider, whereas Bobby had a lithe, lean look about him that she found appealing. His tawny-colored hair reminded her of a lion's mane, partly because he did so little to tame its thick, wavy length.

Once she saw him in daylight she realized that his eyes were actually blue, so dark that she had first thought them black. So what difference did it make, anyway?

Because he's your husband, a small voice whispered.

"Not really."

Legally, morally and in every respect, he is now your husband.

The sound of the bathroom door opening interrupted a scathing retort aimed at her small, inner voice...which was a good thing, because she would have lost her voice at the sudden sight of Bobby walking out wearing nothing more than an inadequate towel draped carelessly around his hips. He was drying his hair with another towel.

"The bathroom's all yours," he said. "Which bed do you want?"

Darned if she didn't have to swallow twice before she could get a sound out of her mouth. "I don't care."

He walked over to the one closest to the window and threw the covers back. She realized that he was going to bed without bothering to dress. Casey darted into the bathroom and closed the door, leaning against it as though she expected him to follow her.

How silly could she be? She got a glimpse of her face and almost laughed. A person would think that she had never seen a nearly nude man before. Actually, that was close to true. Certainly not one in a room they were supposed to share. Somehow beachwear looked fine near the water, but being that close to him had set her nerves to twitching.

He wasn't quite as lean as she'd first thought, at least not in his chest, although his waist and hips were certainly small enough. The muscles in his legs surprised her as well. The horrifying realization swept over her that she wasn't nearly as shocked by his almost nudeness as she was intrigued. She'd wanted to stand there and stare at him. Even more, she'd wanted to touch him. Her fingertips had tingled at the idea of exploring his broad chest and muscled shoulders.

What in the world was wrong with her? Had repeating vows with the man made her lose all her sense?

She was tired, of course, and perhaps a little distraught by all that had been happening in her life. A warm shower would help calm her nerves and soothe her spirit. Following her practical advice, she slipped off her dress and undergarments and stepped into the shower. The water did feel relaxing, she admitted to herself. She allowed her mind to go blank as she absorbed the pressure gently massaging her body.

By the time Casey stepped out of the shower, she felt mellow enough to once again face Bobby. She was relieved to discover that she really didn't have to because he appeared sound asleep when she returned to the bedroom.

Thank goodness. She, too, had forgotten to take anything into the bathroom to wear. She fumbled in the small bag Bobby carried and found the oversize sleep shirt she'd hastily purchased, took it back in the bathroom and pulled it on. The towel had covered her more adequately than a similar one had him, but she was glad he hadn't seen her.

Once again she crept back into the bedroom and peered at the sleeping man a few feet away from her bed. After slipping beneath the covers with a contented sigh, she turned so that she was facing him. He lay on his stomach, his head turned away from her, so that all she saw was his tawny mane of hair and his deeply tanned shoulders. The sheet was draped over most of his torso.

It suddenly occurred to Casey that she felt safe with this man in a way she'd never felt with Steve. She wasn't certain why. Perhaps because he wasn't pretending an interest in her that he didn't have.

No wonder the kiss had confused her, now that she thought about it. It seemed to be out of character for the man she thought she was getting to know.

She turned over and snuggled into her pillow. It felt good to relax after being up all night and most of the day. It also felt good to know that she was now safely protected from having to marry Steve. Despite his brusque manner, Bobby had come to her aid when she needed his help. She would never allow herself to forget it.

Casey was awakened some time later by a resounding swat across her posterior and the words "Rise and shine, sugar. It's time to hit the road."

She forgot all about her gratitude and sprang out of her bed swinging. "How dare you hit me!" she yelled, her fists doubled and aimed for his face.

He dodged her, laughing, his deft footwork keeping him out of her hitting range. "Whoa, whoa there, sugar, now. I didn't mean any harm. I tried every other way I could think of to get you awake. I swear you'd sleep through a bomb exploding right up next to your head."

Casey stopped and looked around. It was dark outside and the drapes were open, the television was blaring, and Bobby was dressed, obviously ready to leave.

"You could have said something," she muttered, "without hitting me."

"I said lots of things but none of it caused a stir."

She rubbed her rear. "That stung."

He fought not to smile but she distinctly saw his lips

twitch. "Sorry," he said as though she was to believe he felt the least bit contrite.

Well, she was certainly awake now, she decided ruefully. Once again she dug in the bag and pulled out one of the new blouses and a pair of slacks and disappeared into the bathroom without another word. Why did the man have to be so blasted irritating?

Bobby waited until the door closed behind her before allowing himself to grin. The gal had spunk, that's for sure. When she finally *did* come awake she'd become a fighting tiger. If any of those swings had connected, he'd have more than a few bruises to show for it.

Actually, he *had* tried to wake her by turning on the television, whistling while he went in to wash his face and comb his hair. She'd really been knocked out. He'd almost been worried that she might have taken some kind of drug and was unconscious, but her last reaction had reassured him on that score.

He had to admit that he'd enjoyed seeing her asleep. Those long lashes of hers were enticing lying on the flushed cheek he could see. She'd looked very demure in her sleep shirt, if he ignored the fact that it showed off her legs once again.

He shook his head. No need into thinking along those lines. What he needed to do now was to get her back home. If they got on the road shortly, they would be back in Texas by late tomorrow morning. Between now and then he needed to find out how she wanted to handle the next stage of their arrangement, because he needed to be heading north as soon as possible.

On the other hand, he didn't want her to feel deserted by walking away from her as soon as they reached her home.

Maybe he should have found out more about what

she intended to do but it was too late now to second-guess what she might have planned.

He walked over to the large window and looked down at the colorful Las Vegas Strip. Too bad they didn't have some time to play. He remembered what the chaplain had said about coming here for their anniversary.

Now that was a laugh. They'd be lucky to be married for a few weeks, much less a year, which seemed to suit him just fine. He was glad that other people he knew had found happiness in pairing off together, but Bobby knew better than to try it. He'd been on his own much too long, was too set in his ways and already had his future mapped out just fine.

He heard the door open behind him. Without turning around, he said, "Come look at the view."

"I thought you were in a hurry."

"You don't have to spend hours admiring the view, sugar. A glimpse might hold you just fine."

"Why are you always so sarcastic?" she asked, walking over to the window and looking down. "Wow," she whispered, already forgetting her irritation. "Doesn't that look like fun?"

"I was thinking the same thing."

"Do we have time to—"

He cut her off. "Not a chance. I've still got to get to Wyoming and that's after returning you to Texas and getting my gear." He turned away and walked over to the bag they were sharing. "You got everything you need?"

She glanced around. "Yes."

"Then let's go."

He could tell from the way her spine straightened that

she did not take kindly to orders. Tough. He wasn't out to win any popularity contests, anyway.

Within the hour they were headed east. Bobby realized that his little bride had a temper that could not easily be ignored. At least she didn't rant and rave and wear his ear off. No, she just didn't speak. Since he was used to being alone, he was kind of accustomed to silence or a radio playing. But there were things they needed to discuss, so he might as well get started.

"What's the next step, Casey?" he asked, breaking the silence that had built between them.

"I don't know what you're talking about," she replied in her most polished tones.

"Well, you said you wanted to get married. We're married. Now what? Do you plan to go back home? If not, what are you going to do?"

Actually, Casey had been asking those very same questions ever since the lights of Vegas had disappeared behind them. There was a sense of anticlimax going on here that she needed to dispel.

If she had gone through with the plans to marry Steve, they would have taken a few weeks and flown to the Bahamas and explored the Virgin Islands. Obviously she and Bobby wouldn't be lazing around in the sun together.

The first thing she needed to do was to contact an attorney and get the paperwork started on her inheritance. She had no idea how long that would take. Despite Steve's remarks, and her father's disdain, she had applied and been accepted at Texas A&M.

Maybe the best thing would be to go to College Station and get set up there. A lot would depend on how her father reacted to her elopement. But then she didn't want him to know that this marriage was just a sham.

Somehow she had to convince him that she and Bobby were going to be setting up housekeeping together.

For that, she would need a visible husband.

"Well," she began, "would it be possible for you to spend the night with me at my dad's ranch?"

He whipped his head around. "Are you out of your mind, woman? I thought this wasn't supposed to be a real marriage."

"It isn't, but that doesn't mean that I want my dad to know that. What would be wrong if I told him that we met some time ago and that you had come back into town and found out I was getting married, and convinced me to run off with you, instead?"

He gave her a sideways glance and shook his head. "I think you've been seeing too many romantic movies, sugar."

"Well, I have to give him some reason why I married you!"

"How about the truth?"

She sighed. "If I tell him the truth, he'll have the marriage annulled and me married to Steve immediately afterward."

"He's really sold on this Steve character, isn't he?"

"I've already explained all of that."

"Aren't we going to have the marriage annulled, anyway?"

"I don't want anyone to know that."

"Oh, great. So I've got to pretend to be married to you even after all this is over."

"Not really. In fact, as far as I'm concerned, you can get the annulment whenever you want. I just need the papers to prove we actually got married, which will be mailed to me as soon as they're filed in the county records."

"Then what's the deal with convincing your dad this is a real marriage? Is he going to insist on escorting us to a marriage bed or something?"

Casey could feel herself turning red. Darn the man, anyway.

"Forget it. I'll tell him you've got to leave right away. I'm sorry I mentioned it."

They rode for another couple of hours in silence. Then Bobby began to laugh.

"What's so funny?"

"We are. I've never argued with a woman as much as I have you. You'd think we'd been married for years the way we go at it."

"For your information I get along with everybody else just fine."

He shook his head. "That's hard to imagine, but I suppose I'll have to buy it if you say so." He glanced over at her. "It seems to me you missed a great opportunity, though. If you'd treated Steve the way you do me, he would have been begging you not to marry him months ago."

"Very funny."

"It's the truth. It doesn't matter what I say, it sets you off."

"It's not just what you say, it's the way you say it. You don't have to act as though you've got all the answers all the time."

"Hell, woman, I don't have any of the answers, any of the time. That's why I was asking what you wanted to do once we get back to Cielo."

"I'll drop you off at the bar and you can take your truck and go wherever you like."

"I thought you wanted me to meet your father."

"I changed my mind."

"What about Steve?"

"What about him?"

"Is he going to believe you got married if you don't show up with an adoring bridegroom?"

"Excuse me, Mr. Metcalf, but I don't think your acting abilities can be stretched far enough to carry off the part. So don't worry about it. I'll think of something when the time comes."

That's what worried him. With Casey Carmichael, an imagination could be a dangerous thing. Just look where it had gotten her so far.

Damn. He was going to have to meet these people and find out why such a fire-eater like Casey would be intimidated by them. He didn't like the idea that either her father or her ex-fiancé might be physically abusive.

She was right. They would handle it when they got back, but she was wrong about doing it alone. If he had to act like a besotted newlywed, he'd do it.

Come to think of it, he decided with an unholy grin, he just might enjoy it. After all, if they were around other people, what could she say or do but to go along with whatever he did.

He certainly enjoyed getting her riled up, that was for sure. She was good in a fight—never pulled her punches and gave as good as she got.

He would never have guessed that he would admire those particular qualities in a woman, much less in a wife.

Chapter Four

How do we get to your dad's place from here?"
Bobby asked the next day as they crossed the county
line into Texas.

"*We* don't. Just go pick up your truck. I've written
my address down for you so that you can stay in touch.
If you'll give me your address, I'll let you know when
I've gotten my trust fund open."

He sighed. "We're talking at cross purposes here.
After giving the matter considerable thought, I think it's
necessary that your father meet me so he doesn't believe
you made all of this up. Remember, you don't even
have a copy of the certificate."

"I do, too."

"Not the recorded one. It won't be here for a while."

"But I've got a copy that has everyone's signatures
and when and where we were married."

"I tell you what, sugar. I'll stop baiting you if you'll
stop arguing with every blasted thing I say, okay? I'm
saying that I think you were right to suggest I go home

with you, stay the night, play the besotted new husband, then give my excuses to everyone about having to be in Wyoming. I'll come back here as soon as I'm through up there, and we'll plan our next step. There's no reason to act like we're complete strangers, now, is there? At the very least, we're partners in this thing. Who knows? We may end up being friends by the time this whole thing is over. Weirder things have been known to happen, you know.''

She stared at him suspiciously. "Why are you suddenly being so agreeable?"

He shrugged. "Because I've had plenty of quiet time these past several hours to think about things. I think you had the right idea all along. What more do you want from me, anyway? I'm saying you were right and I was wrong. Is that so strange?"

She didn't say anything for several minutes. When he looked over at her he saw that she was blinking suspicious moisture away from her eyes while staring blindly out the window. Finally, she said, "To be honest, it is. I'm not used to anyone listening to what I think about most anything."

"Then you'd better get used to it, because we're in this thing together and I'm going to expect you to tell me how you want to handle things, okay? If we don't agree, which seems to be a pattern with us, then we'll talk it over until we find some sort of compromise." He glanced over at her and smiled. "All right?"

"All right," she conceded quietly.

He reached over and patted her knee. "Don't worry, now. You're going to be able to pull this off just fine, 'cause I'm going to be right there beside you all the way."

Casey hoped he remembered his staunch reassurance

an hour later when they pulled into the ranch yard and discovered both her father and fiancé—make that *former* fiancé—standing beside Steve's brand-new, fully loaded, top-of-the-line Bronco.

Before they had come to a complete stop, her father was beside the car and reaching for the door handle on her side. "My God, girl, I've been worried sick about you. Where in the hell have you been?"

Bobby would not have believed it if he hadn't seen it with his own eyes, but Casey seemed to wilt right there in front of him. Her chin began to quiver and her hands shook.

She got out of the car and leaned against it. Bobby had a hunch she didn't trust her legs to hold her. What in the hell was going on here, anyway?

He quickly got out of the car and walked around to where she stood. Holding out his hand to her father, he said, "You must be Graham Carmichael. I'm pleased to meet you. I'm Bobby Metcalf."

Graham ignored him as though he wasn't there. "Answer me, damn it. You've had me half out of my mind for two days and nights! I thought you'd been kidnapped or killed or something. Even Steve didn't know where you'd gone. You've made us both look like a couple of fools, calling everybody we could think of trying to find you. I swear you don't have any sense, whatsoever. I'll be damned glad when you're married and off my hands. I'm sick of trying to keep up with you and your childish behavior."

Without thinking, Bobby put his arm around Casey's waist and drew her up next to him, unconsciously trying to share his warmth with her. She was visibly shaking now, and when he touched her arm, she felt chilled even though the late morning was rapidly moving into the high temperatures.

Steve had followed Graham more slowly, watching what was happening, but when Bobby pulled her into his side, Steve spoke up. "I don't know who the hell you are, nor do I care, but I want you to get your hands off Casey. Now!"

Bobby wondered if she was aware that she actually moved closer to him, if that was possible. All thought of having a little fun with Casey disappeared. He didn't like the look on either man's face. He didn't like the thought that he could have even considered letting her face these two on her own.

Casey hadn't exaggerated the power these two men appeared to have over her. The scrappy feminine creature he'd gotten to know and had found unexpectedly attractive had disappeared without a trace.

And that irritated the hell out of him. Who did these bozos think they were to treat her in such a fashion?

In just a few minutes he was being shown why Casey had run from this kind of intimidation; why she had been willing to approach a stranger to get the help she couldn't find from those who were supposed to be closest to her.

Bobby glanced first at Graham before leveling his gaze at Steve Whitcomb, taking his time to notice the carefully styled hair, the tanning-salon-bronzed skin, the carefully tailored western-cut suit and polished boots.

He already knew what *he* looked like, in his wrinkled shirt, old jeans, beat-up boots and unshaven face. He certainly hadn't come to make any great impression on anyone, which was a damned good thing, he decided ruefully.

Steve's demand for him to let go of Casey still hung in the air.

"I don't think I will, but thanks for the suggestion," Bobby replied quietly. He felt Casey stiffen, but he kept his arm snugged around her, his hand carelessly splayed over her hip in a provocatively possessive manner.

Graham saw that his glaring frown at his daughter wasn't having the effect he'd counted on, so he turned his attention to Bobby for the first time. "What are you doing here and who the hell do you think you are?"

"I'm the man who just may have to teach you how to show a lady some respect, you stupid bastard. Is that any way to talk to your daughter?"

Graham looked startled by the quiet delivery of the inflammatory response. Or maybe he just wasn't used to people standing up to him. Well, he was going to have to start getting used to it. Like it or not, Bobby Metcalf was now part of his family, and he wasn't going to take any guff from this bully. Starting now.

Steve stepped closer as though he was going to physically remove Casey from Bobby's embrace, but stopped suddenly as though he saw something in Bobby's expression that gave him pause.

Making up his mind on the moment, Bobby brushed his lips against Casey's ear and in a low voice said, "Go get as much of your things as you can pack in a hurry. I'm not leaving you here. Do you understand?"

She gave a brief nod and straightened away from him. She circled the other two men, then dashed for the house as though all the hounds of hell were after her.

She just might be right, at that.

Bobby leaned against the car, crossed his arms over his chest and draped one foot across the other before saying, "We can make this little meeting as easy or as hard as either of you two want it to be. It's going to be your call, gentlemen.'' His tone left no doubt that he saw no gentlemen anywhere on the premises.

Graham had been making sputtering noises as he watched his daughter go into the house. "What did you do to my daughter?" he demanded belligerently.

Bobby gave them both a wide grin and replied, "I married her."

He was finding their reactions pretty interesting. Obviously these two men operated in a similar fashion— through bluff and intimidation with anyone they thought weaker. They weren't certain, yet, what category to put him in, he could see that.

He didn't have a problem with that.

So he waited for them to decide.

Steve was the first one to find his voice. "What are you talking about, you ignorant redneck, Casey is engaged to me! We're getting married next weekend."

"Then I guess it's up to me to explain that you're too late, good buddy. As soon as I got back in town and found out Casey was actually engaged and planning to go through with the wedding, I got in touch with her and we had a long talk. Somewhere in that discussion I managed to convince her to go to Vegas and marry me instead."

Both men looked as though they'd been poleaxed and the message hadn't hit their bodies yet. They stood there staring at him, stunned.

"Why haven't I ever heard of you before?" Graham managed to say. "You're talking like you've known Casey for a while."

Bobby continued to smile amiably. "Seems like I've known Casey forever. Brad Bennett and I have worked the rodeo circuit together for years. Whenever we were in town I'd visit his family. As best as I can remember his sister DeeDee and Casey were always underfoot pestering us about something.'' He was really enjoying himself now, just watching the expressions on each man's face. "I promised Casey I'd wait for her to grow up before I married, but what with one thing and another, I guess I didn't show her enough attention or something. When Brad told me she'd gone and gotten herself engaged to somebody else I had to hightail it back here and remind her of her promise to me.''

In a voice filled with total disbelief, Steve said, ''Are you saying that you proposed marriage to a child?''

"Didn't you?" Bobby replied, all trace of a smile gone. "I'd planned to give her time to finish college and see how she felt about things. Now she tells me that you started pestering her while she was only a junior in high school, barely seventeen. Hell, man, she's almost young enough to be your daughter.''

If Bobby had been looking for a fight, he now had one on his hands. Steve lunged for him, ready to trap him against the car. However, Bobby hadn't been around the rodeo crowd all those years without learning a great deal about hand-to-hand combat. The first rule he'd learned was if you're going to fight to win, there are no rules.

So he managed to trip Steve by shoving his foot between Steve's ankles, then as Steve fell forward, Bobby greeted the man's chin with a strong upper cut that started low and had his full weight behind it, knocking the taller, heavier man flat on his back with such force that Steve slid a ways in the dirt.

Although Bobby was convinced he'd just busted three knuckles, he calmly looked at Graham and said,

"You planning to throw your weight around, too, old man?"

Steve pushed up on his elbow and thoughtfully rubbed his jaw that was rapidly swelling. He worked it as though there was a possibility it was broken. Bobby could only hope. He was tired of listening to the jerk.

Bobby wasn't too certain what Graham might have done if the back screen door of the house hadn't slammed, distracting him. Graham turned to see Casey struggling with three large matching pieces of expensive luggage.

Bobby loped over to the porch and grabbed two of them and went back to the car, stepping around Steve who was now up and dusting himself off. He popped the trunk open from the driver's side, threw in the suitcases, then closed it. He met Casey halfway down the walkway and took the third one. "We'll put this in the back seat, sugar," he said smiling.

He turned to Graham and said, "I really hate to break up this touching family scene, but we've got to make tracks to Wyoming right away. I'm entered in a rodeo there this weekend." He opened the passenger door and helped Casey inside. "We'll be in touch."

Graham was already yelling before Bobby could get around the car and inside.

"If you think you can pull this kind of nonsense with me, young lady, then think again. If you leave this property with that man, you're no daughter of mine, do you hear me? Now you get out of that car and get back into the house. You're getting married next weekend to Steve, here, and you know it. I don't know what kind of game you think you're playing, but it's going to stop right now."

Bobby was pleased to see that Casey appeared calm

once again. Not her usual, feisty self, but at least she was no longer shaking.

"I'm going with my husband, Daddy. I tried to tell you several times, just as I tried to tell Steve, that I didn't want to marry him, but neither one of you would listen."

Steve moved gingerly toward the car. "Why didn't you tell me there was somebody else, Casey?" he demanded. "You never once mentioned this character to me."

She smiled. "I know."

Bobby glanced at her. "You ready to leave?" he asked in a low voice.

"It's past time. I can see that now," she replied in an equally low voice. Then she looked at her father and said, "I've always loved you, Daddy, and I always will. But this was one time when I couldn't do what you wanted just to get your approval. I'll write and send you our address."

"Don't bother," he replied coldly, turning on his heel and striding toward the horse barn without looking back.

Steve looked from Graham to Casey, then back to Graham. It was only now becoming apparent to him that he wasn't going to become Graham Carmichael's son-in-law next Saturday. Bobby almost felt sorry for the guy as he watched panic set in at the realization.

Steve turned to Casey and said, "Look, Casey, we can work this out. Maybe I haven't always been real straight with you, but you know I love you. You know I was counting on us being together. You know—"

She cut him off, saying, "Goodbye, Steve. Have a good life."

Bobby thought that was a fair exit line, so he threw

the car in reverse and gunned it, spinning the wheels and throwing up dust. With a sharp maneuver he paused long enough to throw it into low gear and spun the car around so they were facing the road, then took off, leaving Steve standing there in the dust watching them ride out of his life.

Neither one of them spoke until they reached Bobby's truck, which was still sitting where he'd left it, looking undisturbed.

"We need to leave your car somewhere safe for a week or so. Do you have any suggestions?"

She glanced around at him as though pulled out of her own thoughts. Only then was she aware of where they were. "Wha—? Oh! Don't worry about me, Bobby. You've really done enough. I'll just—"

"You'll just stop arguing with me for once, how about it? I know this wasn't what we planned, but I think it's a good one. You come to Wyoming with me. Once I'm through there, I have some spare time. We'll take you down to College Station and find a nice apartment for you. I'll rent it in my name in case anybody bothers to check. I'll also keep in touch and make sure you're doing all right. I don't think you need to be on your own for a while. I'm not too sure what either one of them might come up with once they've had time to face these new developments. I don't want you anywhere around."

"But I need to have the recorded license and the clerk is supposed to send it here."

"I'll call them right now. They're just barely open back there. I'll give them my post office box number. It should be back by the time we are. You'll be fine."

He didn't like the way Casey looked at the moment.

She was much too pale. Her eyes looked glazed. She was definitely in shock.

"How about your friend, DeeDee? Could we leave the car with her?"

She sat there in silence as though she hadn't really heard him. When she answered, it was to say, "My father has never cared anything about me. Why haven't I faced that before? I've tried and kept trying to be what I thought he wanted but it was never enough. And now..." she paused and took in a ragged breath, "Now I've finally done the unforgivable and I can't feel a thing." She looked over at him, her eyes wide, the pupils dilated. "Isn't that weird?"

It was at that point that the walls around Bobby's heart cracked wide open and he let another person inside. He reached for Casey across the console that divided the bucket seats of her car. "It's going to be okay, Casey. I promise. You aren't alone. You've got me, for what that's worth. At the moment, it isn't a lot, I've gotta admit. I've been a rodeo bum for most of your life, and mine as well, collecting few possessions because I wanted to travel light. But I stand behind my word. I will be there for you and take care of you. You don't have to battle this thing alone."

He thought for a moment that she was going to allow him to comfort her, but no. He could already feel the stiffening in her spine pulling her away. She ignored everything he'd just said. Instead, she answered his first question.

"I know DeeDee will keep the car at her place. She can put it in the barn until we get back. If you don't mind, I'd like to go with you. I've never been to Wyoming." She sounded like a stranger making polite conversation.

Maybe that was the only way she was going to be able to handle their present situation, which was fine with him. He appreciated her control since he seemed to be losing his. His emotions had suddenly taken over his thinking. Bobby had never felt so confused, so overwhelmed, in his entire life.

"Fine," he said as nonchalantly as possible. "I'll follow you to her place, then we'll go pick up my horse and rig at the fairgrounds and hit the road." He gave her a mock punch to the jaw. "I think I'd sleep a little better tonight if we were somewhere north of here."

She managed a smile before slipping out of the car and walking around to where he waited for her.

When they arrived, Bobby was pleased that her friend DeeDee didn't seem surprised at Casey's request, but seemed to be overjoyed when Casey shyly admitted that they had run off and gotten married. She let out a whoop and danced around the yard, holding on to Casey's hands and laughing.

"Wait until I tell Brad. He's not going to believe this. Bobby Metcalf ran off to Las Vegas and got married—again!"

Bobby rolled his eyes but didn't say anything. What was there to say, after all?

It was Casey who stopped DeeDee with, "Please don't tell anyone. Please. I mean, we want to keep it a secret for a while. I'm going to college the way I planned and, well, Bobby is going to be busy with the circuit, and—"

"But what about Steve? Aren't you going to tell him?"

"Oh, we've already told Dad and Steve."

"Wow! I'd like to have been there to have seen

that,'' DeeDee said, her freckled face glowing with animation. ''What did they say?''

Casey glanced around at Bobby and he waited for her to respond. He almost laughed out loud when she said with great dignity, ''I don't believe they were pleased,'' which he found to be such a wonderful understatement that *he* wanted to grab her and twirl her around the yard in a laughing, dancing jig.

After giving DeeDee a quick hug and promising to be back in a week or two for her car, Casey crawled into the cab of his dirty truck and looked around with interest.

Bobby was embarrassed. The truck looked to have been well lived in, since it was the only home he really had, except for his post office box in the town where he'd grown up. None of his family was alive now, but he'd never seen a reason to change it. He rarely got mail, anyway.

''Sorry about the mess,'' he said, pulling out of the driveway and onto the street. ''I'll clean it out when we get to the fairgrounds.'' He had a camper on the back of the truck where he kept a sleeping bag and where he'd put her bag. She'd left the other two in her car, for which he was thankful.

He wasn't used to traveling with anyone, but he sure as hell wasn't going to leave her alone. Not after that last scene.

So instead of pulling into a roadside rest area after dark as was his usual practice, once they crossed the Kansas line he opted for a modest motel. They had spent most of the day in a silence that seemed to be a continuation of the one that had accompanied them from Nevada. He kept an eye on her without being obvious and could tell that, although she was fighting it, Casey was exhausted.

He had her shower first, so that by the time he was through with the bathroom, she was asleep. She'd picked the bed next to the wall, leaving him the one by the window and door.

Bobby made certain that the chain lock was in place before he, too, turned in, flipping the light switch off. He quickly drifted off to sleep, since he'd driven the entire night before, and it was only later that a slight noise awakened him to immediate alertness…until he realized that it was Casey.

In the deep shadows of the room he could see her huddled figure, her face buried in her pillow in an effort to muffle her sobs. It was obvious that she didn't want him to know she was crying, and he decided to respect that by not saying anything or moving over to comfort her. Instead he lay there, listening to the deep pain she expressed in the only way she knew how, feeling absolutely helpless.

Bobby knew that from this moment on he would never look at himself or his life the same way again. There was someone else in his life now, someone young, too young to be placed in such a vulnerable position. She deserved so much more than what she'd experienced thus far in her life.

She deserved someone a hell of a lot better than him, for that matter. But at the moment he was all she had, and he was determined not to ever let her down.

Chapter Five

Four Years Later

Casey hurried across campus on a Friday afternoon in early May, already late for her last class of the week. She'd gotten so absorbed in her lab class that she had lost track of time. She glanced at her watch as she jogged to the next building, shaking her head in exasperation.

As soon as she stepped inside, one of the professor's aides saw her. "Oh, there you are. I was just going to your class to give you this." She handed Casey a note.

Impatient with the interruption, Casey quickly unfolded the note and read the short message. Frowning, she glanced up at the aide. "Are you sure this is for me?"

"Yep, they said Casey Carmichael."

"But I don't know anyone in Fort Worth. Why would the hospital there want me to call them?"

The girl shrugged. "Who knows? Maybe a family member had an accident there."

Casey froze. "Did they give a name?"

"Nothing. You're to ask for Ms. Sanchez at that extension number," she said, pointing to the information on the note.

Well, that certainly did it for making today's class. "Is it all right if I use the phone in here?" she asked, pointing to one of the offices.

"Sure. Go ahead."

If anything had happened to her father, he wouldn't have been hospitalized in Fort Worth. Besides, she would be the last person he would want called if he were ill. He hadn't spoken to her since she'd driven out the driveway four years ago, despite the fact she occasionally wrote him in an effort to stay in touch.

There had been a lot of water under the bridge since then, but her father was legendary for holding a grudge. Especially when he didn't get his own way. Very few people had dared to defy Graham Carmichael. He certainly wasn't going to forgive his daughter for managing to get away with it.

She punched in the numbers of her credit card on the telephone, then the numbers jotted down on the note. When the hospital answered, she dutifully gave the extension number. As soon as a voice answered, she said, "May I speak to Ms. Sanchez, please."

"This is Ms. Sanchez."

"This is Casey Carmichael at College Station. I have a message to call you."

"Yes, Ms. Carmichael. Your husband was admitted to the hospital earlier today. He was involved in an automobile accident. His vital signs have stabilized. We'd like you to come to the hospital."

Puzzled, Casey replied, "I'm sorry, but there seems to be some mistake. I'm afraid you've reached the wrong person."

"Mr. Robert Metcalf lists you as next of kin, ma'am. That's all we have to go by."

"Robert Metca— Oh, my gosh! You mean Bobby's been hurt? What happened? How bad is he?"

"He's in stable condition at the moment. We'd appreciate your coming to the hospital."

"Oh. Well, thank you," Casey said slowly, hanging up the phone.

"I hope it wasn't bad news," the aide said when Casey walked out of the office.

Casey felt shaky, suddenly, and very unsure of herself. Bobby was in the hospital in Fort Worth and they wanted her to come. What could she do? What was expected of her?

She remembered the aide's question. "Uh, yes, I'm afraid so. A friend of mine was in an auto accident."

"If you would like, I could notify the instructors that you've been called away on an emergency."

The aide's calm response helped Casey to focus. "Yes, I'd appreciate that very much. Thank you."

She left the building and headed for her car, her thoughts jumping in all directions.

Of course she would go to Fort Worth. Was Bobby asking for her? What did it mean that she was listed as his wife? Surely he would explain that—

Then it hit her. He must be seriously hurt, maybe unconscious. Stable condition didn't tell her how badly he'd been hurt. If he was unconscious he wouldn't be able to explain to the nurse that she wasn't really his wife.

Not now, anyway.

But there had been a time, oh, yes, there had been a few months when she and Bobby had been legally wed, husband and wife. She would never forget that summer after she'd graduated from high school when her life had changed so completely. Nothing had ever been the same again.

She pulled into the driveway and hastily parked, then ran into her apartment. It was the same one that Bobby had leased for her that fateful summer—another reminder of the impact he'd had on her life—and feverishly began to gather some clothes into a small bag. She had to think about what she would take and for how long. Only then did she realize that she didn't have a clue where to find the hospital once she reached Fort Worth.

She dug into her handbag where she'd absently stuck the message and once again dialed the hospital. After getting directions she hung up, decided on a three-day wardrobe and finished packing.

Within the hour, she was headed north, still driving the red roadster her father had given her for her graduation present. She'd seen no reason to trade it in, since she hadn't really put many miles on it, not after that jaunt to Vegas.

She always smiled to herself whenever she thought about that wild trip and its consequences. At least one thing had gone as she had so naively planned—she'd received her grandfather's inheritance, once she was able to produce the marriage certificate.

As promised, she'd notified Bobby when she received the money and offered to send it either to his post office box or directly to a bank. In response, she received a blistering telephone call reminding her in no uncertain terms that he had told her more than once that he did not want her money, he had never wanted her money, and that he didn't want to hear any more about her money. Her memory had already deleted the obscene adjectives he'd used to describe said money and his pithy comments suggesting exactly what she could do with it.

However, a promise was a promise as far as she was concerned. It wasn't the first time she'd disagreed with Bobby Metcalf, and if she was going to be seeing him again—which looked to be the case—then it was a safe assumption that it wouldn't be the last time.

So she had instructed the attorney to place the money in an interest-bearing account in his name and to send Bobby the passbook.

She could be just as stubborn as he was.

Of course he had called her to say that she could put it in his name, but there was no way in hell he would ever touch a penny of it. She calmly pointed out that he was being terribly shortsighted, but if he was determined to do without money that he certainly deserved, there was nothing she could do about it.

She wondered now if he'd ever decided to use it, or whether the sizable amount was sitting in the bank somewhere building interest.

Casey realized how much she was looking forward to seeing him again and prayed that he wasn't seriously hurt. Obviously it was serious enough to have him hospitalized. She could only hope it was for observation or just to be on the safe side.

She couldn't picture Bobby in a hospital. He was too vital, too energetic, much too restless.

That summer she'd spent with him had given her a fairly good idea of his character, his nature and his personality. His plan to get her settled in College Station had been sound. It had actually happened. But not in the few days he'd first suggested.

She had ended up traveling with him for weeks, so that she was given an opportunity to observe rodeo life, firsthand, not to mention the teasing Bobby received once Brad spread the news that Bobby had eloped to Las Vegas with a girl he'd just met.

He'd surprised her by not visibly reacting to all the ribbing he got. Instead, he calmly introduced her around, made certain she was well looked after and went on with his contests week after week.

He even showed a rather gratifying affection toward her when anyone else was around them. When they were alone, though, he fell into the habit of treating her like a pesky little sister. She hadn't minded, at first. As a matter of fact, she'd found his casual attitude toward her a relief while she adjusted to all the changes that were taking place in her life.

For one thing, she hadn't really thought her father would actually write her off so quickly or easily, and it had been devastating for her when she discovered that he had no intention of even speaking with her, going so far as to hang up as soon as he heard her voice on the phone.

She was glad that Bobby had been there, helping her work through her shock and despair with his casual acceptance of her in his life.

She'd also been grateful for Bobby's rather primitive way of making his point the night that Steve showed up at one of the rodeos a couple of weeks after she'd married Bobby. Steve had been by turns cajoling and threatening toward her, insisting she end her marriage with Bobby and come back to him.

All it took was for Bobby to suddenly appear—she

never knew who told him that someone was there heatedly talking to her—and Steve suddenly remembered a very pressing engagement elsewhere.

What a jerk he had turned out to be. The smartest thing she had ever done was to refuse to marry him. The person she was today would have stood up to him from the beginning. The person she was today wouldn't have needed to marry Bobby or anyone else as a form of protection.

The person she was today had slowly evolved as a result of the trauma she'd experienced back then. It had taken her some time, but she had managed to grow up. A large part of that was due to Bobby Metcalf.

There might have been an entirely different ending to that part of her history if it hadn't been for Bobby. However, Casey found it really tough being grateful to someone who could, depending on some personal whim of his that she'd never been able to figure out, irritate, aggravate and incense her as much as he could.

She couldn't help but wonder if the personality clash they used to have had changed in the years since she'd actually seen him.

She had a hunch she was on her way to find out.

Once Casey reached the city limits of Fort Worth she followed the instructions she'd jotted down and soon found the hospital. She sat in the car for a few minutes after having found a parking place, realizing that she was really afraid to go inside and find out just how badly he'd been hurt.

Never in a million years would she admit it to him, but she had formed a great deal of respect for the man. She'd found an acceptance from him that she'd never before experienced. She had told herself during these past few years that Bobby was the brother she'd never had, determined to ignore the strong sexual attraction that had sprung up so strongly the only time he'd ever kissed her.

"Please, God, please let him be okay," she whispered, then stiffly stepped out of the car, her muscles protesting the hours spent sitting behind the wheel.

At the information desk in the front lobby she was directed to the medical wing. After reaching that area, she approached the nurses' station.

"May I help you?" one of them asked.

"I'm here to see Bobby Metcalf. Could you tell me how badly he was hurt?"

"And you are—" the nurse asked, waiting for identification.

"Oh! I'm Casey Carmichael. Someone called me to say that Bobby had been brought in as a result of an accident."

The nurse picked up a chart and opened it, then glanced up at Casey. "Mrs. Metcalf, your husband hasn't regained consciousness since the accident. However, his vital signs continue to be stable. The doctor has diagnosed a concussion, two broken ribs and fractures of the tibia and fibula of the left leg. In addition, he's being observed for possible internal injuries."

Casey closed her eyes for a moment. It was worse than she'd hoped. At least the unconscious part explained why he hadn't told them the truth about them, that their marriage had been annulled years ago.

She was still glad that she had come. "May I see him?" she asked.

"Yes, of course."

The nurse gave her his room number, and Casey went down the hallway to the designated door. After taking a deep breath, she pushed the door open and stepped inside. Her gaze immediately fell on the motionless figure lying on one of two beds in the room. The other bed was empty.

She quietly made her way to the bed and stared at the man who lay there. Thick lashes rested against his cheeks. She hadn't remembered that about him, but she recognized the high cheekbones and strong, stubborn jaw. Although his skin was still deeply tanned from the sun, there was no healthy glow about his color beneath the bruises that were becoming apparent.

She touched his hand, running her fingers lightly across his knuckles. She hated seeing him this way. She wanted him to open his eyes and give her that no-nonsense glare of his.

"Hello, Bobby," she managed to say in a hoarse, emotion-filled voice. "I wish I knew what I could do to help you. I came as soon as I heard."

As though through the magic of her wish, Bobby's lashes fluttered, then slowly opened. He stared at her blankly, without focusing.

"Hi, there," she said softly. "How are you feeling?"

His lashes fluttered as he murmured a word in the form of a question. "Maribeth?"

Casey immediately recognized the name. It was the woman he was supposed to have married. Had he thought that was who Casey was? She had never seen a picture of the woman. Perhaps they looked alike, or perhaps he had been dreaming of her.

The door opened behind her, and Casey turned to see the nurse she'd spoken to earlier.

"He just opened his eyes," she told her.

"Yes, we picked up heightened vital signs on the monitor. Did he say anything?"

"A name is all."

"Did he recognize you?"

"I don't think so."

The nurse checked him and spoke to him, trying to get him to respond. He moved his uninjured leg and moaned. The other leg was in traction.

The nurse looked at her and smiled. "I believe he is rousing. I'll let the doctor know." She had already reached the door before she said, "There's a couple in the waiting room asking about him. I told them you were with him and they asked to speak with you when you were available."

Casey immediately followed the nurse out into the hallway. After the waiting room was pointed out to her, she went down the hallway and paused in the doorway.

She couldn't remember when she'd ever seen a more attractive couple. The man fit the description of tall, dark and knockout handsome, while the woman, with her red hair and porcelain complexion, was drop-dead gorgeous.

Casey cleared her throat, and the man, who'd been pacing the floor, saw her and asked, "Were you with Bobby Metcalf just now?"

"Yes. I'm—"

"How is he? Nobody will tell us anything. If I didn't have a friend who caught his name on the police radio band earlier today, we wouldn't have known anything about his being taken to the hospital."

"He's been unconscious, but seems to be rousing, and the nurse has gone to let the doctor know. She said he has a concussion and some broken ribs, plus his leg is broken in two places."

The woman had jumped from the chair where she'd been idly thumbing through a magazine when Casey walked in and joined them. When she heard Casey's report she let out a little cry of dismay. The man immediately put his arm around her in comfort. Then he turned back to Casey.

"I'm Chris Cochran and this is my wife, Maribeth. We grew up with Bobby. He called last night to say he'd be heading our way—we live in Dallas—and was going to stay with us tonight. Then I got this call about an accident here in Fort Worth and that Bobby was listed as one of the survivors."

Maribeth. So this was the woman Bobby had almost married. Casey wasn't certain why she had such a sense of dismay to discover the gorgeous creature before her who might have married Bobby all those years ago.

"Hi," she said, forcing a smile. "I'm Casey Carmichael. Bobby has told me about you. It's nice to finally be able to put faces with names."

After a brief hesitation Maribeth replied, "I'm afraid you have us at a disadvantage, then. Bobby has never mentioned you to us, but the nurse said you were his wife."

Her comment held more than a hint of a question.

Oh, dear. Casey really didn't want to get into explanations, particularly to close friends of Bobby's who he had obviously not told about her. However, she had to say something. After a moment her thoughts zeroed in on a possible explanation. "I'm not certain what happened. Maybe Bobby carried old identification. Maybe he didn't think about updating whatever information he carries. I don't understand it, either. I mean, we were only married for a—"

"Then you *are* married to Bobby," Chris exclaimed, frowning. "I wonder why he never mentioned it to us. When did all of this take place, for God's sake? Why haven't we met you before, for that matter? You've never been at the ranch when we visited.''

"The ranch?''

Maribeth looked at her suspiciously. "You don't know about Bobby's ranch? And you're married to him? That's all he's been able to talk about during the eighteen months since he bought the place.''

"Well, you see—'' Casey began, when the nurse who'd spoken to her earlier walked up and spoke.

"Pardon me for interrupting. I just wanted to let you know that I managed to catch the doctor while he was still here on rounds. He's going to check your husband and speak with you in a few moments.''

Casey nodded. "Thank you. These are close personal friends of Bobby's. I know he would want to see them if he knew they were here.''

The nurse smiled. "You'll need to check with the doctor on that,'' she said, and walked away.

Casey turned back to the couple standing there. "I'm as confused as you are that the hospital thinks Bobby and I are married.''

"But *you* said you were married,'' Maribeth said.

"But only for a few months. Bobby was supposed to have the marriage annulled. I just assumed that he did.''

Maribeth looked at Chris with an expression Casey didn't understand, then turned to her and asked, "When, exactly, did you and Bobby get married?''

Chris laughed and said, "C'mon, honey. Casey isn't old enough to have been the one he ran off with and married in Las Vegas back then. This young lady was probably still in grade school.''

Casey could feel herself blushing. Why, she couldn't say. She was still unnerved to discover these friends of Bobby's had never heard of her. But when she thought about it, she guessed there was no good reason for Bobby to have ever mentioned her.

"Four years ago. However, after that first summer we didn't stay in touch." Thinking of their news, she added, "I'm glad to know he got a ranch. He used to talk about getting one someday." Maybe he finally stopped being so stubborn and used the money she'd sent to him, she thought to herself.

"If your marriage was annulled," Maribeth asked, "why are you here?"

"Well, the hospital called me. They said I was listed as next of kin and asked me to come. I was more concerned over his condition than I was about their getting our marital status right."

"Mrs. Metcalf. I'm Dr. Johanson," said a man who walked up. "I believe your husband is regaining full consciousness. However, due to the nature of his injuries, it isn't surprising that there is some confusion. I think seeing a familiar face might help him at the moment."

She really didn't want to go into the fact that Bobby would have no reason to find her familiar. Instead she said, "I'd like his friends to come, as well. They're very close, and I know he would want to see them."

The doctor looked at the other two. Whatever he saw seemed to reassure him. He nodded his head and said, "All right."

As they walked down the hall, the doctor filled them in on the details of Bobby's health. By the time they opened the door, he concluded with, "Now that he is showing signs of rousing, I'm much more optimistic about his general condition."

Casey felt very uncomfortable at the moment. She was there under false pretenses, after all. Once inside the room, she moved reluctantly toward the side of the bed.

Bobby turned his head when the door opened and watched them come toward him. He didn't say anything.

Since the other three looked toward her, Casey obediently went to the side of the bed. "Hi, Bobby. How are you feeling?"

His eyes seemed to search her face, feature by feature. The growing silence increased her discomfort. Finally he said, "Like I tried to ride one too many bulls," he muttered.

Chris, Maribeth and Casey laughed out of relief. This sounded like the Bobby they all knew.

The doctor was watching him intently. "Does it help to have some familiar faces around?" he asked quietly.

Bobby cut his eyes around toward the doctor without moving his head. "Are you saying I'm supposed to know these people?"

There wasn't a sound in the room now. It was almost as though the three visitors had sucked in air and forgotten to release it.

"Do you recognize your wife?"

Bobby closed his eyes, then slowly opened them and looked at the three people standing nearby. "I have a hunch it's not the tall dude. I don't remember being married at all. How could I remember a wife?"

They looked at the doctor in concern. His expression revealed nothing. He just nodded and made notes on the chart, as though what Bobby was saying was perfectly normal.

Casey had expected him to at least *remember* her, even if he wasn't particularly pleased to see her. How could he not recognize the two people he'd grown up around?

Chris stepped forward. "You must have gotten a hell of a blow. Do you remember how the accident happened?"

Once again Bobby closed his eyes. Without opening them, he said, "I told the doctor. I'm telling you. I don't remember anything. Nothing. Nada. Zip. Is there anybody around this place who can understand me? Hell, I didn't even know my own name until I heard someone call me Bobby."

Chapter Six

Casey, Chris and Maribeth sat at a corner table in the hospital cafeteria trying to eat while they discussed Bobby's condition.

"It breaks my heart to see him this way," Maribeth said.

"Dr. Johanson said it isn't that unusual for head injuries to cause confusion," Chris replied. "Remember, Bobby was unconscious for several hours."

Casey let their discussion wash over her without making an effort to join in. She felt drained of all energy and overwhelmed with the present situation.

What should she do? Hang around the hospital until Bobby remembered that he didn't even know her? Explain to the doctor the mistake made when she was called?

Maribeth broke through Casey's reverie by saying to her, "Look, why don't you come home with us tonight? We'll return tomorrow. Hopefully by then he'll be feeling better. There's nothing more any of us can do tonight. It isn't as though we can comfort him in any way. I'm sure he's in a great deal of pain and prefers not to let what he considers strangers know about it."

"Knowing Bobby," Chris added, "he wouldn't admit to pain to his closest friends, which I suppose happens to be the three of us."

Once again Casey felt like a fraud. She had been waiting for some pointed questions from these two regarding her marriage and why it had ended, but after their first questions, they had been tactfully silent on that score. There was no way she could accept their friendly hospitality.

"Thank you, but I think I'll stay in a motel close by so I can come back early. I'm embarrassed that he probably won't remember who I am, even when he does recover his memory, but I feel as though I need to be here, anyway."

Chris grinned. "Oh, I don't think Bobby has married so many times that he generally forgets the women he's loved and left."

"Chris!" came a wifely rejoinder. "He's seriously hurt. How can you joke at a time like this?"

"Because the doctor assured us that he seems to be out of the woods and appears to be recovering nicely. What's wrong with a little amnesia among friends? There's actually something to say for a little selective amnesia, you know."

"It isn't funny," Maribeth insisted.

"I never said it was. I'm just saying that Bobby is recovering. He's going to be okay. And it's my strong belief that he's too damned hardheaded to have permanent damage. This is the guy who rode bulls for a living. He went out looking to get hurt!" He patted Casey's hand. "You do whatever makes you most comfortable. We'll come back over here tomorrow, probably in the afternoon. By that time, maybe he'll be his usual, rip-roaring self.''

Later that night Casey lay in a motel bed, staring at the darkened ceiling. This was the first motel she'd been in since the summer she'd spent with Bobby. It seemed fitting, somehow, to be here because of him now.

She recognized that she was almost too tired to go to sleep. This had happened to her before, during final exams at school last year, where her mind had whirled at night with miscellaneous thoughts and refused to shut down.

Today had been so strange. She recalled waking up that morning with no inkling of the startling message that would send her away from her round of classes and throw her back into her past. Life could be so strange, sometimes, and change could come without warning.

She sighed and turned over, burrowing her head into the pillow. Perhaps tomorrow would bring some sense of closure between her and Bobby, she hoped. Eventually her body won the struggle, and she drifted off to sleep.

For the next few days and nights Bobby faded in and out, unsure when he was dreaming or awake. The nurses seemed to come in to check on him whenever he had finally become comfortable enough to sleep. He fell asleep at odd times, dozing most of each day, being awake most of each night.

By the end of his third night in the hospital, various memories began to surface, mostly disconnected pieces of information, but at least he began to get a sense of who he was and how Chris, Maribeth and Casey came to be in his life.

The toughest part was remembering Casey. No wonder she'd continued to be so quiet around him. She had to be confused that she'd been called on as his wife.

Once he recalled the reason she was there, he was furious at himself for carrying her name on his ID. The last thing he ever wanted was to find Casey Carmichael at his bedside while he was so helpless. This accident had destroyed his hopes to eventually convince her he wasn't a rodeo bum.

Bobby fell back to sleep as the sun appeared on the horizon.

Chris walked into Bobby's room several days later mid-morning. Bobby was lying in bed after having been out, moving around the room with the assistance of a nurse and a walker. The little bit of exercise had exhausted him, causing his head to throb more than usual. It irritated him to be so weak. All that movement hadn't helped ease the pain in his ribs, either.

"You look like hell," Chris said, dropping into a chair. "What's going on?"

"They had me sitting up for a while last night. This morning I had to test out the cast, make certain I could get around with it."

"Too bad you don't have your memory back, or you'd recall how many casts you've worn over the past several years."

Bobby looked at him with disgust. "Oh, most of my memory is back. Doc said it wasn't unusual to have some confusion after a severe blow to the head. I'm not saying I can remember everything, and I still don't remember the accident, but most things seem clear enough."

Chris jumped from the chair and in a couple of strides

was at the side of the bed. "Well, hell, Bobby, why didn't you say so as soon as I walked in! That's great news, buddy. I don't mind telling you that we've all been really worried, even though we didn't want to let you know how concerned we were."

Bobby looked at his friend without saying anything for a moment. Slowly he smiled. "Is that why you came in so casual, like we'd just been out painting the town the night before, and I was still hungover?"

Chris laughed. "Yeah. Casey and Maribeth will be delighted to know that you're doing so well. Which reminds me," he said, drawling his words. "Isn't there a little something you forgot to mention to us, Bobby, my boy? Like another wedding that nobody knew about?"

Bobby looked past him to the door, then asked, "Where are the women?"

"Maribeth took Casey shopping. It seems she only brought a few things and has now run out. They told me to come on up and visit with you and they'd be here later."

Bobby could feel himself relaxing at the news. He wasn't certain how to face Casey, or what to say to her.

"I never mentioned the marriage because it was never a real marriage in any sense of the word."

"Oh, I don't know. We've had time to visit with Casey while we were waiting on you to wake up and join us. According to Casey, the two of you managed to tour most of the western states together the first summer of the marriage." Chris raised an eyebrow and said, "You haven't forgotten that little bit, have you?"

"She was just a kid, Chris, barely eighteen. She had no idea what she'd gotten herself into. Her dad kicked her out and she had nowhere else to go, at least until time to go off to college. I never took advantage of the situation. Just kept her with me, made certain she was all right, then took her over to College Station and found her a place to live. Hell's bells, Chris, I haven't seen her in four years.''

''That's what she told us. So why are you carrying identification that says she's your wife if the marriage was annulled?''

Once again Bobby took his time answering the question. Not that he felt the need for secrecy where Chris was concerned. Chris and Maribeth were his closest friends. He probably should have told them about the marriage, about his future plans, hopes and dreams. The thing was, he'd never really cared about what anyone thought of him, never cared about his reputation—until Casey came into his life.

Once she was at school, he'd taken stock of his life, where he'd been and where he was going, and he hadn't liked what he'd seen. He liked to think that meeting Casey had made him want to grow up. About time, too. He was pushing hard onto being thirty-four years old. Chris and Maribeth had been married for eight years, had two kids and a great life, while he was still trying to put his life into some kind of perspective. He hadn't been comfortable attempting to explain his feelings until there was reason for him to believe that he and Casey might have a future together.

Now that whole idea was laughable.

''The thing is,'' he began a little haltingly, ''I told Casey I'd see to the annulment. I had her sign the necessary papers but I never actually filed them.''

''Which means you're still married to her.''

''Yeah.''

''Why?''

"Because Casey was the first good thing that had happened to me in a long time, and I didn't want to lose her."

"According to what you just said, you never *had* her to lose. Since she wasn't aware that she was married, what did you intend to do if she became serious about someone else?"

"A friend of mine lives down that way, and he used to keep an eye on her once in a while for me. He'd take snapshots of her when she was on campus. She made lots of friends at school, but she's really serious about getting her education and that didn't leave much time for a social life."

"You're still as crazy as you always were," Chris said with a grin. "Why couldn't you just tell her how you felt and let nature take its course?"

"Because I don't want her to know how I feel. I don't want her to feel obligated to me in any way. If she became interested in anyone else, I planned to file those papers without her ever knowing the truth. It was just that I had hoped— Well, it doesn't matter anymore, does it?"

"I don't know. What had you hoped?"

"Talking about it makes it really sound like a cowboy's drunken fantasy. I used to sit around thinking about how much I enjoyed her company that summer. She was really something—despite all she'd gone through with her dad and that creep he had picked out for her—she worked to put all of that behind her.

"She impressed the hell out of me. Once she was gone, I kept thinking about what her dad had said about me. He called me a rodeo bum...and he was right. That was all I was when we met.

"So I decided to change all of that. I stopped spending money on anything but my bare necessities. I put myself in a rigorous training program. And it worked. I started winning more purses. When I found the ranch, I thought I was on my way to proving myself. I figured I had a few years to pull everything together. She was always determined to become a vet, and that takes years of training. I had some time to get the ranch going, where it would be paying its own way. By the time she would be ready to set up a practice, I thought I'd be able to look her up, casual like, and maybe get a chance to show her that I could be the man in her life that she could depend on to look after her. Maybe date her...spend time with her...let her get to know me as I am now."

Bobby couldn't believe that he was spilling his guts like this. He'd never talked so much in his life. He'd kept these feelings bottled up for years. Now that he was putting them into words, he knew that he'd never stood a chance of pulling any of this off. He'd just been kidding himself.

"It doesn't really matter, anyway. Even if I could have pulled that off, there's no way she's going to be interested in a broke, ex-rodeo bum hobbling around on crutches."

Chris had listened quietly while Bobby had rambled on. Bobby was surprised that he was more relieved than embarrassed to have shared his fantasies with his best friend. It had helped him face the truth a little easier.

Chris cleared his throat, then said, "You know, Bobby, I think you could make all of this work in your favor if you handle it right."

"What are you talking about?"

Chris stood and walked over to the window, glanced outside, then turned back to him. "Well, I've been watching Casey closely since we met her. I wanted to understand what had attracted you to her in the first place—besides the obvious, of course,'' he added with a grin. ''The thing is, I would say she cares a great deal about you. Much more than you seem to think. It was obvious to the most casual observer that she was upset when she arrived to learn that you had been injured. She's also concerned about your lack of memory where she is concerned. There's a lot of unfinished business between the two of you that was raised when she discovered you carry ID naming her as your wife and next of kin.''

Bobby groaned.

''You could make this situation work in your favor, you know,'' Chris continued, ignoring Bobby's response. ''It wouldn't take much to convince her to go back to the ranch and look after you until you get that cast off.''

''Damn it, Chris, that's the last thing I want! I don't want to be helpless around her, for God's sake. I wanted to convince her that I could look after her, not the other way around.''

''That will come eventually, Bobby. Give all of this some time. In the meantime, let her go to the ranch and see what you've been working to build there. I think she'll be impressed. Let her get to know you again.''

''And how do I explain the ID I carry on me?''

Chris grinned. ''That's the beauty of the situation. You don't have to, not right away. You've had some serious injuries. Your memory is still playing tricks on you. You've got the perfect excuse not to answer questions you aren't ready to deal with. Instead, use the time to recuperate and at the same time, let her get used to being in your life once again.''

"Every penny I've earned is sunk into that place, Chris. I found out yesterday my truck was totaled. Not that it was worth much, but it got me around. I don't know how I'm going to replace the thing."

"Since the accident wasn't your fault, you can rest assured that the insurance company will get you some wheels. I can guarantee it. In the meantime, here you are, no memory, broken bones, no transportation—"

"I have a memory, you numbskull, weren't you listening? Or are you rapidly losing yours?"

"Oh, I remember. However, only you and I know your memory's back, right?"

Bobby wondered if maybe his brain wasn't functioning as efficiently as he'd thought. Chris wasn't making any sense.

"I told the doctor this morning."

"No problem. We just won't tell our ladies the truth for a little while. That way, Casey will feel that she is starting over with you since you don't remember her or the particulars of your marriage. It will give you both a chance to start over. You'll be able to buy some valuable time with her, which is what you've been wanting, anyway. Right?"

"I don't like lying to her."

"You won't have to...unless she continues to ask you about your memory. You can have it come to you gradually, remember your childhood first, that kind of thing. She can't hold you responsible for not telling her you're still married to her if you don't remember that part of your life, now can you?"

"You are a devious man, Chris Cochran."

Chris stood beside the bed, looking at Bobby in silence for a lengthy pause. "You're in love with her, aren't you?"

"I never said that," Bobby shot back defensively.

"You didn't have to. I recognize the symptoms, having suffered from unrequited love for many years until you got out of my way and gave me a chance with Maribeth."

"And that's another thing. If you'd been up front about your feelings for her, things could have worked out a lot easier for all of us back then."

"It was her feelings for you that I couldn't discount. I always knew that you loved Maribeth in your own way, but mostly you loved her because she had always been a part of your life and tagged along behind you. You took her for granted. I wasn't all that surprised that you ducked out of a wedding back then. It was Maribeth's feelings that had to be considered, and you hurt her really badly."

"You think I don't know all that? Why do you think I'm so worried about hurting Casey now? I never wanted to hurt Maribeth, but I did a damned good job of it. Let's face it. I don't know anything about making a relationship work. I've never been any good at talking about my feelings."

"You made a good start this morning, Bobby. The world didn't come to an end, now, did it?" Chris chuckled. "You've got a chance to go after something you truly want. Don't get cold feet at this point. After all these years, you've finally met someone who is important enough to you to cause you to change habits of a lifetime. You want a chance with her, don't you? Well, here it is. Take it. This situation can be made to work for you if you'll swallow your pride a little and let her look after you for the next few weeks."

Bobby considered his friend's advice. He had to admit that Chris had a point. Of sorts. The problem was that Bobby had never had anyone to look after him since he was a kid. He'd been on his own a long time.

He didn't like being fussed over. But it was true that he was going to need some help in the coming weeks. He had Slim at the ranch, who could do the necessary outdoor work, but Bobby kept up with his own meals and any housecleaning that might get done.

He flinched at what he remembered his place looked like.

He'd planned on doing some remodeling to the house as soon as he had the extra money and before he invited her to visit him.

He was still mulling over Chris's suggestions when the door opened and Maribeth and Casey walked in.

Once he'd recognized them he was amazed and a little amused at how similar the two women were in appearance. Casey's hair was more reddish blond than Maribeth's defiantly red hair. Their eyes were light, and they were both tall. He had never given the similarities between the two a thought until now.

He noticed that Casey hung back whenever she came to visit him with anyone else, as though she were shy, or as though she wasn't certain of her welcome.

He still hadn't decided what to do about her when Maribeth asked, "How are you feeling today, Bobby?"

"Better. The doctor said I could probably be released by the weekend if I continue to improve."

He could have wrung Chris's neck when he said, "You can't go back to the ranch alone, Bobby. I'm sure the doctor is assuming that your wife is going to be there to look after you, but as we explained to you yesterday, she's been away at school and hasn't been living at the ranch."

Casey immediately stepped closer. "I'm almost

through with the school year, Bobby. After my finals next week, I'll have my degree. I was going to take some summer classes, but I can always postpone them.'' She'd been talking quickly, as though expecting him to interrupt her. Instead, he was watching her closely, and she could feel her self-consciousness grow. In a rush, she added, "I'll be glad to stay at the ranch with you…that is, if you want me there.''

"Of course he'd want you there,'' Chris quickly replied before Bobby could say a word.

So there it was, laid out for him. All he had to do was to agree to have her at the ranch. He could still tell her that he now remembered everything. All he'd have to do was to explain about the annulment papers. He'd had a good reason for not filing them immediately after she'd gone back to school. He could explain all of that to her, couldn't he? He'd have some time, maybe, to come up with a reason that they were still married today, if he gave it some thought.

Swallow his ego and let her look after him, huh? Was that all it took?

This certainly wasn't the way he'd wanted things to be, but this was the hand he'd been dealt, so he might as well play it out and see what happened.

"If you're willing to come, Casey, I'd like to have you there,'' he finally said and was surprised to see her blush a rosy color.

Chris was right, damn him. He was in love with this woman, really in love for the first time in his life. This just wasn't the way he'd planned to court her.

He suddenly remembered a sign he once saw that read, "If you want to see God smile, tell Him your plans.''

He had a hunch that God was grinning mighty big these days!

Chapter Seven

This was not the way that Bobby had planned to return home, he thought disgustedly as he lay in the back of Chris's minivan like some kind of invalid.

He supposed he should be grateful that Chris had offered to drive him the four hours from Fort Worth to San Saba county. It was a hell of a lot cheaper than an ambulance would have cost.

What was it with these doctors, anyway, that they didn't understand a man could survive with one leg in a cast without being pampered to death?

It didn't help matters any that Chris found this whole situation so blasted amusing. What kind of a friend would get such a charge out of seeing someone struggle to make some sense out of his life?

"You okay back there?"

"I'd prefer to be sitting up there," Bobby replied, doing little to hide his irritability at his situation.

"The doctor said you needed to keep that leg elevated,'' Chris said, his gaze meeting Bobby's in the rearview mirror of the minivan.

"What does he know?" Bobby muttered.

"At least we know that blow to your head didn't knock any sense into it," Chris said, grinning. "For some reason, I find that rather comforting. A totally reformed Bobby Metcalf would be too much of an adjustment for me to have to make."

"The doctor kept me almost a week longer than he first said," Bobby complained. "I should have gone home last week."

"And paid for it with swelling in that leg and more problems with your head. Give it a rest, Bobby. At least they released you today. Of course, that was probably because every nurse that had to look after you was begging the doctor to get rid of you."

Their gaze met in the rearview mirror and they both laughed.

"Probably. All I know is that it will be good to be home," Bobby admitted wryly. The conversation lapsed and Bobby closed his eyes, just for a few minutes, or so he thought. He must have drifted off to sleep because the next thing he knew the door beside him opened and Chris was peering down at him.

"C'mon, cowboy, you're home," Chris said, his voice tinged with concern. "Think you can make it inside without help?"

Bobby sat up and looked around. The late afternoon sun hovered above the western hills, which meant that he must have been asleep for several hours.

Well, so much for thinking he was recovering rapidly. A simple little ride home had practically knocked him out. He must be getting old.

He glanced at the house and saw Casey and Maribeth

come out the kitchen door and down the steps toward him.

"I'd offer to help you out," Chris said, smiling, "but I know what that would do to your macho image, old man."

Bobby fumbled for his crutches and carefully got out of the minivan. The fact was that he'd had too much practice over the years getting around on the damned things and he didn't need to be reminded of that particular skill at this particular moment. So he ignored Chris's remark and started toward the house. He was greeted at the steps by both women.

"How are you feeling?" Maribeth said, her sympathy obvious.

Casey just stared at him with wide eyes.

"I'm okay," he said. "Relieved to be out of the hospital." Negotiating the steps on crutches took his total concentration. Nothing more was said until he reached the porch level and found Chris holding the screen door open for him.

As soon as Bobby was inside, Casey said, "Your bed's ready for you."

Bobby scowled at no one in particular. "I'm not going to bed. I've spent too much time in bed, already." He continued through the kitchen without looking at any of them, headed toward the hall door.

Chris spoke up quickly. "Does anything look familiar to you around here, Bobby?"

Bobby stopped as though he'd run into a wall. He looked around and saw the three of them staring at him in concern.

Hell. What was he supposed to say? That he remembered leaving the place a few weeks ago? Only then did he notice how clean everything looked. He sighed. "I have a hunch this place has never looked so clean."

His remark eased the tension when the others laughed. Chris seemed to be pleased with his response and came to his rescue. "Why don't you go into the living room. The couch in there is long enough for you to stretch out. Just remember to keep that leg elevated to prevent swelling."

"Gee, do you think I can find the place without help?" he asked, turning away and making his slow way down the hallway.

Casey hadn't moved from her position just inside the kitchen door to the porch. She wasn't sure what to do now that Bobby was actually there. It was one thing to volunteer, in theory. It was another thing entirely to be faced with the reality of their situation.

Maribeth must have seen her uncertainty in her face because she spoke up. "I don't envy you having to put up with him in his present mood," she said ruefully. "It's difficult being hindered, particularly for someone as active as Bobby."

Casey appreciated Maribeth's matter-of-fact comment. It helped her to remember that Bobby's mood had nothing to do with her. "That's true," she replied. "I was laid up last year when a horse stepped on my foot. I definitely remember being a real grouch by the time the cast came off."

Chris stood with his hands in his pockets and looked around the room. "Bobby was right. You two have really been working in here. The place doesn't have quite so much of a bachelor pad feeling." He nodded to the countertop that was no longer littered with tools and other odds and ends.

Casey smiled. "It's obvious Bobby spends very little time in the house."

"Typical rancher mentality," Maribeth said. "We take care of our stock better than we do ourselves."

Chris glanced at his watch. "I hate to be a spoilsport here, honey, but we need to get on the road if we're going to get back home tonight."

Maribeth turned to Casey. "Are you sure you'll be all right, looking after him on your own?"

"I'm not completely on my own, you know. He's got two ranch hands out there I can call if I need any help."

Chris walked toward the hallway. "Then I'll go tell the grump that we're heading out of here. If you manage to put up with his moods without choking him in the first twenty-four hours, you'll deserve a medal, at least."

Casey watched Chris as he disappeared down the hallway, then turned to Maribeth with a smile. "I don't know how to begin to thank you for all your help and support since the accident. I don't know what I would have done without you and Chris these past few weeks."

"We were glad to do it. Bobby is family, even if we aren't blood-related. Besides, I'm glad to have the opportunity to meet you. Frankly, I really admire your willingness to stay here, given the fact you've been out of touch with him for so long and he has no memory of you."

"It's enough that he's accepted the fact I've been away at school without questioning why I would leave him alone so long."

"At least his extra week in the hospital gave you time to finish out the year. I understand you begin veterinarian school in the fall, right?"

Casey glanced toward the door that led to the living room. "That's the plan, although I haven't discussed it with Bobby. I've tried to keep everything in the present for now. Who knows? Once he's on his feet and regains his memory, he'll recall what a pest I was back when we first married. He'll probably be glad to see the last of me." Casey was pleased that she sounded as though she didn't care one way or the other. She didn't want anyone to know how strongly her feelings had been stirred since Bobby had reentered her life so abruptly.

"He's already remembering lots of things, which I think is a good sign," Maribeth said.

Casey nodded. "Mostly about growing up in Agua Verde. Although he made a couple of references to the ranch last week that made me think he may be remembering it, as well."

At that point Chris returned to the kitchen and they went outside. With a flurry of hugs and best wishes, the Cochrans waved and got into the minivan.

Casey stood on the porch and watched them drive away, feeling more than a little abandoned despite her reassurances to them. She felt as though she had a half-tamed savage in the other room that she was supposed to understand and assist, if he'd allow it. She didn't want to fight with him, not in the way she had done four years ago. Instead she wanted to show him how mature she'd become since she'd been that eighteen-year-old pleading for his help. Too bad he couldn't remember her back then.

Sighing, she turned and went back into the house. From the kitchen she could hear the sound of the television broadcasting a news program.

Well, standing there in the kitchen wasn't going to get her anywhere. Casey forced herself to walk into the other room. Bobby glanced up from the television as soon as she paused in the doorway.

"So, I guess it's just you and me here, now," he said with a hint of wariness.

"Guess so."

He leaned his head back on the pillow behind him and with a half grin said, "You don't have to hover in the hallway, you know. I don't bite."

So much for hiding her nervousness from him. With a sense of irritation at her own shyness, Casey walked into the room and sat down in one of the chairs arranged across from the sofa.

Silence reigned supreme for several minutes. Finally, Casey asked, "May I get you anything?"

"You're my wife, not my servant, Casey," he muttered irritably.

Casey counted to ten, then tried again. "Did the doctor give you anything to take for pain?"

He touched his shirt pocket. "Yeah."

Wow, this was fun, she decided. Bobby had never been much for talking, but this was really ridiculous.

"How was the trip home?" She was determined not to sit there until bedtime without talking.

He ran his hand through his hair, shifted the leg that was encased in a plaster cast and said, "Okay, I guess. I slept most of the way."

She smiled at his tone. "You don't have to sound so disgusted, you know. Rest is the best thing you can do for yourself right now."

He looked down at his leg, then away. "Lucky me."

Casey leaned forward in her chair. "Actually, you were very lucky. Your injuries could have been much worse."

He sighed, leaned his head back and closed his eyes. "I don't like feeling helpless."

"Now there's a piece of shocking news. I never would have guessed."

Without opening his eyes, he said, "Tell me about school. Do you like it?"

She reminded herself that he didn't really remember her. He was probably hoping that something she said might trigger a memory of their life together. She felt guilty for not telling him that in the past four years, they'd only lived together for a few weeks.

However, Chris had pointed out to her that the doctor didn't want Bobby to get upset, not with the head injury he'd suffered. For some reason she didn't quite understand, Chris had thought Bobby would be more comfortable with the idea that they were actually married, rather than practically strangers. Bobby would probably have refused to have her there, if he knew the truth.

This was the first time they'd spent more than a few minutes alone since his accident. It was only natural that he would have some questions. There was no reason for her to be nervous, she knew. Nevertheless, she was as tense as she'd been taking her finals.

"I enjoy school," she finally said in reply. "There are some classes I enjoy more than others. I guess that's natural."

He seemed very sincere when he looked at her and said, "I'm sorry I was in the hospital and missed your graduation. That's something to really celebrate."

She could feel her face grow warm. "Actually, I skipped the actual ceremony. I told them there was an emergency in the family. The school is mailing me my diploma."

Feeling more relaxed by his willingness to have an

ordinary conversation with her, Casey hoped that the tension between them would continue to ease. She was also pleased to learn that he approved of her efforts, even when he didn't remember her or their relationship.

"It must feel strange to find yourself married to a stranger," she said. From his sudden frown she realized his lack of memory was a touchy subject. Quickly she searched for a change of topic, and launched into a funny story one of her professors had told her class recently. She felt rewarded when he laughed out loud, only to groan and rub his side.

She jumped up from her chair and knelt beside the couch. "Oh, I'm sorry, Bobby. I forgot about your broken ribs."

"It doesn't matter. They'll heal." He eyed her a little uncertainly. "It feels a little strange to me, having you here like this." He reached out and stroked her hair back behind her ear. "But I'm glad you're here. I want you to know that."

Her heart started thumping hard against her chest. What had she been thinking, moving over here to him? She looked up at him and saw him watching her intently.

"You seem a little uneasy around me," he said softly. "Any particular reason?"

"We haven't spent all that much time together, actually," she said.

"Was that because you were in school, or was it something more than that?"

She could sure use Chris's advice now, she thought. "Does it really matter, at this point?" she responded, feeling a little desperate. "I'm here now, and that's what really counts."

He leaned over and brushed his lips softly against hers. "I agree," he said.

She was getting in over her head quickly. Casey scrambled to her feet and said, "I, uh, have to check on the stew I made earlier. If you'd like, I can bring you some in here, so you don't have to get up."

Not giving him a chance to respond, Casey hurried out of the room, leaving Bobby alone.

He stared at the television screen without seeing it. What did he think he was doing, anyway? For that matter, why hadn't she brought up the fact that she'd signed annulment papers?

He couldn't get over the changes in her. Four years had made a big difference in her demeanor. She was more confident, which pleased him no end. She wasn't as argumentative, which was a nice switch, and she turned him on like no woman he'd ever known before.

His body didn't seem to care that he had broken bones and healing bruises, or that the headache that was never completely gone had returned with a throbbing vengeance. Despite all his aches and pains, he wanted to make love to her, which was really a dumb idea, everything considered.

It was enough that she was here in his home, pretending to be the wife he was pretending not to remember. What a farce. However, he might enjoy watching how this one played out.

Would she be willing to stay here and make their marriage a real one? Even if she stayed, he couldn't afford a wife. Not at the moment, at any rate.

What a mess. He was encouraged to believe he might have a chance with her. Someday soon he'd have to tell her about their legal status. She must believe they weren't married, and as long as he didn't let her know the truth, he thought he could deal with the situation. Regardless of how much he wanted to make love to her, he wouldn't take advantage of her willingness to be there.

But there was nothing wrong with kissing her once in a while, was there?

Despite his aches and pains, Bobby couldn't remember a time in his life when he'd been happier. Casey Carmichael had that kind of effect on him. He was almost afraid to hope that everything would work out for them.

Whatever the outcome, he was determined to do what he could to have her permanently in his life.

Chapter Eight

It took Casey a long time to get to sleep that night. She had helped Bobby get ready for bed, determinedly ignoring the sight of his mostly bare body, which still carried the remains of the bruising he'd suffered. He really was lucky to have survived without more serious injuries.

When she'd leaned over him to adjust his pillow, he'd slipped his hand around the back of her neck and pulled her down to him, his mouth seeking hers as though his actions were the most natural in the world. She could have pulled away, of course, but she hadn't. Instead, she braced her hand next to his head so her weight hadn't touched him and shyly returned his kiss. She wasn't going to pretend that she didn't enjoy it, particularly after the teasing kiss he'd given her earlier in the living room.

He took his time, as though learning the shape and texture of her mouth. When he finally eased his hold on her, she drew away breathless.

"Goodnight, sugar," he finally said, his voice gruff. "Thanks for your help. Once I get used to the cast, I'll probably do just fine."

She could only nod numbly and back out of the room. Sugar. He'd called her sugar, the nickname he'd given her when they'd first met. Was he beginning to remember her? Would he recall the real reason they had married? That it hadn't been a mutual attraction that had somehow gone sour as he seemed to believe?

She was surprised that he hadn't asked more about how they had met, how long they dated...things like that. Maybe those memories were surfacing, but if they were, he hadn't acknowledged them. He hadn't been surprised when she had left him and gone into the second bedroom to sleep.

Shouldn't he have at least asked why she wasn't sleeping with him? Didn't he care? She had no idea what she would have done or said to him if he had asked her to stay with him. She was a little alarmed to discover that she wouldn't have automatically told him no.

For the truth was that she very much wanted to make love to Bobby Metcalf. By the end of their time together the first summer, she had wished more than once that he would show some sort of interest in her.

Instead, he had continued to treat her like a sister that sometimes got on his nerves. They had never discussed that aspect of their relationship, other than also referring to the eventual annulment. Obviously they both had known that the only grounds for an annulment was if the marriage wasn't consummated.

Now, of course, there was no marriage, despite his having some kind of identification showing her as his next of kin. He probably hadn't cleaned out his wallet in years. Once his memory returned, she would discuss it with him in a calm, rational manner. Until then, she would have to keep in mind that she was only pretending to be the wife he didn't remember.

There was no reason to ever let him know how she felt about him. It was just a silly crush she'd developed at a time when she'd been very vulnerable. She was no longer vulnerable. However, the crush was going to take a little longer to overcome.

She stared at the open bedroom door. She'd left his door open as well, in case he needed anything during the night. He really hated being dependent on her, she could tell.

He'd gone to bed with very little protest, the dark shadows beneath his eyes revealing the strain he was under. She'd insisted he take the pain tablets he'd been given. After some grumbling, he'd finally complied.

Now if she could just relax enough to drop off to sleep herself.

Instead her mind kept returning to the many fantasies she'd indulged in during her years in college whenever she'd felt alone and unloved.

She would play out different scenarios—such as, what would have happened if...

If she and Bobby had actually made love that summer they had spent together, would he have changed his mind and wanted to stay married to her?

If she had gotten pregnant?

If she hadn't gone on to college, would they have stayed together and built the ranch together?

Silly fantasies, but she finally drifted off to sleep, playing them out in her head.

* * *

The next morning Casey was in the kitchen when she heard a vehicle drive up outside.

She paused and looked out the window. Bobby was standing outside the barn door with Slim watching the pickup truck race across the ranch yard and abruptly pull up beside one of the fences nearby. Casey watched as a dark-haired woman jumped out of the truck and raced over to where Bobby stood, leaning on his crutches.

She wore a bright red blouse and snug-fitting jeans that showed off a curvaceous figure. At the moment she was giving a great impersonation of a boa constrictor that had found its prey, wrapping herself around Bobby despite the fact he was balanced on crutches.

Not that Casey cared, of course. Bobby Metcalf had his own life here, after all. It was nothing to her what he did or who he knew, and if that woman didn't come up for air soon, they were both going to lose consciousness from lack of oxygen!

Casey turned away, having finished the breakfast dishes, and marched down the hall to Bobby's bedroom. She'd put off coming into his room but she needed to make the bed and gather up his towels and— She lost her train of thought when the faint scent of Bobby's aftershave seductively tugged at her senses.

The scent immediately reminded her of their few weeks together, when they had shared space in small motel rooms. She had sometimes watched him shave, teasing him about trying to work around the slight indentation in his chin without cutting himself.

He would give her an exasperated look in the mirror and ask her if she didn't have anything better to do than to hang around pestering him. Generally, she had assured him that she didn't.

But that had been years ago, when she'd been a mere child. Now, of course, she was much more mature. She had learned a great deal about life. She knew how to—

Who *was* that woman outside?!

After hastily making the bed and putting out fresh towels, Casey gathered up the damp towels and raced back to the kitchen and the small room nearby where the washer and dryer stood.

She peered out the window but couldn't see anyone…just the truck still sitting there.

Which meant the woman was out there somewhere.

With Bobby.

Of course Slim was out there, too, she thought, just as she spotted Slim walking out of the barn with a slight wave to whoever was inside. She heard him call to Pablo who stepped out of one of the smaller buildings. The two of them got into a dilapidated truck parked beneath a nearby shed and drove off, following the narrow lane that led to the rest of the ranch and disappeared into the hills.

So now Bobby and that woman were in the barn alone.

Since Casey couldn't think of anything else she needed to do in the house until it was time to start lunch, she got a sudden urge to explore the ranch buildings. She'd been too busy yesterday to do more than glance at the place, knowing that Bobby would soon be arriving from Fort Worth.

With grim determination she strode back to her bedroom, picked up her hairbrush and began to vigorously brush her hair. She'd had it cut last year to shoulder length, so it no longer went into a braid. She carefully swept it to the nape of her neck and fastened it with a hairclip. A nice, sedate hairstyle, befitting her adult status.

Then she peered into the mirror. She looked pale, especially around the eyes. Quickly she brushed mascara on her lashes, then slightly darkened her brows. A hint of lipstick wouldn't hurt, either.

Her jeans looked serviceable enough, and her blue chambray, Western-cut shirt would do for now. With one last sweeping glance at her image in the mirror, Casey marched back down the hall, through the kitchen and out the back door.

The ranch yard appeared deserted.

She might as well start with the barn, she decided, her actions suiting her decision. She reached the barn door and paused, looking into the gloom.

There were several horse stalls along one side, with windows that let in the sunlight. She heard a snuffling, shuffling movement that sounded familiar. That's right. He said he had a couple of horses. He hadn't mentioned what kind.

She entered the barn quietly, not wanting to startle the horses.

"Oooh," said a soft voice, denoting obvious pleasure.

Casey stiffened.

"Oh, Bobby," said the same voice, crooning. The voice sounded muffled. There was a murmuring of something Casey couldn't quite hear, then the words, "Such a darling."

Casey didn't know what Bobby Metcalf thought he was doing out here, but she was here to see that he take care of himself. Her pace had picked up until she reached the couple who were now in one of the stalls.

They had their backs to the stall door, their arms around each other's waist and were looking at—

A foal that couldn't be more than a few days old, nuzzling his mother for nourishment.

Bobby suddenly glanced over his shoulder and saw her standing there watching them. He made no effort to move away from the other woman who had taken the place of his crutches. Instead, he just nodded and said, "Hi, Casey. Did you want to see the newest arrival on the place?"

It was the other woman who spun away, causing Bobby to sway before he caught the side of the stall for balance. She faced Casey, demanding, "You didn't tell me you had company, honey. Is this your baby sister?"

Casey bristled at the sudden amusement on Bobby's face. She wasn't *that* young, for Pete's sake, that she could only be somebody's baby sister.

Now that she was closer, Casey could see that the woman with Bobby was probably his age or close to it. She was attractive enough, Casey decided with a completely neutral detachment, if you liked the voluptuous type.

Compared to her, Casey could pass as Bobby's baby brother!

"Casey, I'd like you to meet one of my neighbors, Frankie Castillo. Frankie, this is Casey Carmichael."

"Frankie?" Casey repeated faintly.

"It's really Francesca," Frankie said with a sideways glance at Bobby. "Frankie is a private nickname Bobby gave me."

"I see," Casey replied, not certain exactly what she was seeing or what it meant.

"I just heard about Bobby's accident this morning from one of the ranch hands who'd heard it from

Pablo," Frankie said. "I was furious that Bobby hadn't called to let me know what had happened." She turned back to Bobby and stroked his arm. "I would have come to the hospital immediately."

Bobby glanced down at his feet. "Well, I, uh—"

Casey spoke up. "Oh, didn't he tell you? Bobby got a pretty hard blow to the head that knocked him unconscious. He was out for hours. And when he came to he didn't remember anything."

"Oh, Bobby, how horrible! No wonder I didn't hear from you. But you're better now?"

He glanced down at the cast on his leg. "Well, once I get this thing off, I'll be a lot happier, let me tell you."

"Oh, honey, I can see that. I meant your poor head." Frankie ran her fingers through Bobby's tawny hair, gently massaging his scalp. She went up on tiptoe and kissed the side of his mouth, leaving yet another slight trace of lipstick on his face to go with other smudges that she had no doubt placed there earlier. "That must have been so awful for you," she crooned in the same tone that she had earlier used for the new foal.

The mare was growing restless and stamped her feet, startling the foal into moving closer to his mother.

"C'mon," Bobby said, pushing the gate open. "Let's get out of here." He reached for the crutches leaning against the side of the stall.

Frankie stepped out beside Casey and extended her hand. "I'm pleased to meet you. How do you happen to know Bobby?"

Several possible responses flitted rapidly through Casey's mind. Hadn't she just been cataloguing all the ways she had matured in the past few years? There was absolutely no reason to make trouble for Bobby. None at all. So she was just as surprised as the other two were when she smiled and cordially shook Frankie's hand before saying, ''Oh, I married him a few years ago.''

Chapter Nine

Before the stunned couple in front of her could respond to her comment, Casey smiled at both of them equally and said, "I just came out to tell you that there's fresh coffee, if you'd like some. Besides, you're not supposed to be up on that leg if you don't want the swelling to come back."

Casey turned and hurried out of the barn like a fox being chased by hounds.

He was going to kill her, she was certain. The look of shocked surprise on his face had only been equaled by the look of sheer horror on Frankie's. So why had Casey said that?

Of course it hadn't been a lie. That was how she'd met him. And now there seemed to be some confusion over the status of their annulment. She recalled that Chris had asked her if the papers had ever been filed. The truth was, she didn't know.

If for some reason Bobby had never gotten around to

making the annulment official, then they were still legally married.

That thought didn't upset her quite as much as she thought it might, considering that she had just that morning been reminding herself that she had a career to plan.

If they were still married, wouldn't that change things?

Would there be any repercussion from her mentioning the matter to Frankie?

She slammed into the kitchen and began hastily to make a new pot of coffee before Bobby made it back to the house. Well, if they were still married it certainly wasn't *her* fault. She had carried out her side of the bargain, after all. If he hadn't carried out his—well, then he deserved to be embarrassed in front of Frankie-Francesca, the sultry neighbor.

So there.

She had an almost ungovernable urge to stick out her tongue.

So much for mature behavior.

Baby sister, indeed.

She heard them coming up the steps, their voices low and intimate, a hint of laughter between them. Casey pulled out the pan of brownies she'd made yesterday and placed them on a serving plate. She was busy setting out coffee mugs when Frankie opened the screen door and allowed Bobby to swing through on his crutches.

"I think your warning may have come too late," he said, grimacing. "I may have stayed up too long as it is."

Casey turned from the cabinets without fully meeting

his gaze. "Why don't you go on into the living room and stretch out on the couch? I'll bring in a tray."

"Can I help with anything?" Frankie asked.

"Just entertain Bobby," she said, much as a mother might mention a fractious child.

"Thanks a lot," Bobby replied irritably.

Frankie laughed. "I'll certainly see what I can do." She walked ahead of Bobby, looking over her shoulder. "Any suggestions on how you want to be entertained?" she asked archly, no doubt knowing how those tight jeans clung to her taut buttocks and emphasized the slight sway of her walk.

Casey suddenly noticed that she was grinding her teeth and immediately turned away from the spectacle.

Thank God the coffee was finished. She poured the coffee and set two full mugs on a tray along with the brownies and followed the other two into the living room. Frankie was busy stuffing a pillow beneath Bobby's head.

"It's his foot that needs to be propped up." His booted foot was still on the floor, while the foot on the leg with the cast was covered with a soft moccasin.

Frankie obligingly slid a pillow under that foot, as well. "The cast is so light. They make them differently these days, don't they?"

"For which I'm eternally grateful," Bobby replied, allowing a soft sigh of relief to escape him.

Casey could have wrung his neck for going out this morning, but she'd known there was no way to stop him. He had to be the most stubborn person she'd ever known. He'd said he just needed to speak to Slim for a few minutes, but he'd been outside almost an hour before Frankie arrived.

Now he was paying for it.

Served him right, she thought, wishing a pang of compassion hadn't hit her when she'd seen the pain reflected in his eyes. Why did he have to pretend to be so tough?

She guessed it was because he *was* tough. Some of the tales that Chris and Maribeth had shared about his past injuries had curled her hair. He'd never gotten hurt while she'd been with him, other than bruised up a couple of times, and whenever she'd shown concern, he'd brushed her fears away with some noncommittal comment.

She was glad he wasn't riding those bulls now. She couldn't have stood it, knowing the dangers. Before, she'd been too ignorant and naive to fully comprehend the dangerous risks he took.

It was a wonder he hadn't broken his neck.

"Bobby tells me that you're going to A&M," Frankie said.

And at the same moment Bobby asked, "Where's *your* coffee?"

She ignored Bobby and answered Frankie. "That's right. I'm starting vet school this fall."

Frankie continued to sit on the couch close beside Bobby's hip. She reached for a cup and carefully handed it to Bobby. "Can you drink this in that position?" she asked, frowning slightly.

He eased himself up a little, and she immediately pulled another pillow out and propped it behind him. "That's fine," he said. "Thanks."

Casey began to back out of the room. "I need to start lunch, so if you'll excuse me, I'll just—"

Bobby interrupted. "You'll get a cup and join us. There's no rush about lunch. It's barely ten-thirty in the morning."

"Oh! I guess I didn't realize—mmm, well, if you'll excuse me, I'll just go get my cup."

She dashed out of the room, her face burning. What was the matter with the man? She was giving him every opportunity she could think of to be alone with his friend.

Instead of turning into the kitchen, Casey continued down the hallway to her room, but not before she heard Frankie and Bobby burst into laughter, enjoying something.

Were they laughing at her? Any why shouldn't they? She was being ridiculous.

She couldn't help but wonder what sort of explanation Bobby had made to Frankie after Casey had fled the barn. Whatever he'd said, she deserved it for putting him in a position to have to explain.

Neither one of them appeared bothered, at any rate. She was the only one who was too embarrassed to face them. She went into the tiny half bath off her bedroom and splashed cool water on her face. She could get through this, after all. She'd done it to herself, even though she must have been hoping to provoke Bobby.

She couldn't imagine why.

By the time she returned to the living room with her cooling cup of coffee, the conversation had turned to what was going on at Frankie's dad's ranch.

Once Casey was seated, Frankie explained, "I moved back home after my divorce last year. I don't know what I would have done without Bobby for company." She stroked his arm. "He helped me save my sanity."

"Don't be silly," he said. "I didn't do anything."

"You listened...and listened and listened. You didn't judge. You didn't try to fix me. You just listened and let me get all of that hurt and anger out."

"I'm not in any position to judge anybody, Frankie. If it helped to talk, I'm glad I was available."

She lifted her brows slightly. "Just not quite as available as I assumed you to be, that's all." She glanced at Casey. "If you're looking for advice, Casey, then I'll warn you that you shouldn't leave this good-lookin' husband of yours alone for long periods of time. Somebody just might come along and snap him right up before you know what happened."

From where she sat, Casey could only see Bobby's profile, but she did notice a slight ruddiness on his high cheekbones. "I'll certainly keep your advice in mind," she murmured before taking a sip of her coffee.

"Are you going to be up to coming to the barbecue, honey?" Frankie asked Bobby. "You know how long Daddy's been planning this little get-together. He'd be so disappointed if you weren't there."

He wouldn't be the only one, Casey thought to herself. With neutral detachment, of course.

"I can't make any promises at the moment," he replied. "But that's almost two weeks away, so there's a good chance I'll be getting around a little better by then."

"I'll be glad to sit out the dances with you," Frankie said in a low, seductive voice.

Interesting how his cheeks seem to grow even redder, almost as though he'd been out in the sun too long, Casey observed dispassionately.

Bobby changed the subject, asking about some of her father's stock, and the rest of the conversation stayed impersonal. When Frankie said she had to go, it was Casey who walked her to the door and waved her off, both women insisting that Bobby needed to stay where he was.

As though he'd been waiting to hear the screen door close behind her once she stepped back inside the house, Bobby called, "Casey? May I speak to you for a minute?"

She closed her eyes and gave a brief prayer requesting mercy even though she knew she didn't deserve any. But God *was* merciful. Maybe He would help her get through this.

Casey entered the living room once again. "Yes?"

He patted the space recently vacated by Frankie. "Sit down, would you?"

"Well, I, uh— You know, I really need to—"

"I won't take up much of your time," he said, not sounding particularly friendly.

She sat down where he had indicated and waited.

She studied the pearlized snaps on his shirt, following the path they led to his throat, before slowly raising her gaze to his slightly indented chin, his sensuously shaped mouth, his nose, and his dark blue eyes that were intently focused on her.

"Yes?" She sounded cool, calm, and collected. Not at all the way she felt.

"What was all that about?"

"What?"

"Don't play innocent with me, sugar. You know exactly what I'm talking about. Why did you tell Frankie we were married?"

"Because we were!"

"Uh-huh."

"And until you can remember everything—"

"Oh, I can remember everything just fine."

She looked at him suspiciously. "Really? Since when?"

"I told you last night, my memory has been coming

back steadily after the first few days I was in the hospital.''

"So you remember why we got married."

"I do.''

She almost giggled at his response, more out of nervousness than anything else. He just sounded so solemn, as though he were still repeating vows.

She shrugged. "Well, then, you didn't need to ask me about it last night, did you?''

"I was curious what you would say. If you'd be honest enough to admit that you had come looking for a man you'd never met in order to propose marriage.''

"Well, then, let's talk about honesty here. It doesn't sound as though you've been particularly honest with me, either.''

"Meaning?''

"Did you ever get the marriage annulled?''

"I, uh—'' He stopped speaking and just looked at her.

"The question calls for a simple yes or no.''

"There is nothing 'simple' about our situation.''

"Care to explain that?''

"Are you aware that your dad was checking up to see if we'd actually gotten married and that he was going to have it annulled so that you couldn't claim your inheritance?''

She stared at him in shock. "But I got the money, don't you remember? We had that big argument on the phone. Surely you haven't forgotten that!''

"The reason you got that money that you were so eager to toss away—''

"I didn't toss it, as you very well know. I had an obligation that I was fulfilling and I fulfilled it.''

"I remember all your irrational explanations very

well. We don't need to go over them, although you ought to know that the money is still sitting in the account where you put it, waiting for you. I've never touched it!''

"My God! But you are absolutely the most pig-headed, mule-stubborn man I've ever known in my life!''

"Add liar to the list while you're at it,'' he said quietly.

Well, that certainly got her attention. "Liar?''

"That's right. When your dad came looking for me and told me he was having the marriage annulled, I laughed in his face and told him to try it. That you and I had lived together as man and wife all summer, and there were all kinds of witnesses to prove it. The funny thing was that he actually hired someone to interview various people on the circuit that year. I guess everyone was convinced that you and I were quite a romantic couple because I never heard anything more from him.''

"You mean you told him you'd slept with me?''

"That's what I'm saying, sugar.'' He laughed without sounding particularly amused. "My virgin bride. Just don't let your daddy ever find out or he may try to take you to court for falsifying documents in order to claim your inheritance. He didn't seem above trying to do that. Sure holds a grudge, doesn't he?''

Casey nodded absently, still caught up in what Bobby was telling her. She'd never known a thing about all of this. Her father had actually—

"Then we're still legally married?''

"Yep. I figured I'd wait until you finished your schooling to tell you. Of course if you'd shown any interest in dating I would have mentioned it sooner.''

"How do you know I haven't been dating?" Even she could hear that she sounded just a tad hostile.

He cleared his throat. "I have a friend who lives down that way. He sort of kept tabs on you for me."

"Sort of?"

"That's right. He wasn't stalking you or anything."

"You could have told me all of this before, you know."

"I thought about it. Decided not to."

She jerked away from him and stood. "That really stinks, Bobby, you know that? I had a right to know what my father was up to. I can't believe you didn't tell me! Was that your idea of protecting me? Well for your information I don't need your protection!"

"Maybe not now," he agreed quietly, looking up at her. "But at the time I thought you did. I happen to know how much you suffered from how your dad treated you. I didn't think it would make you feel any better knowing he was still trying to block you from getting your education, from having the kind of life you wanted. Isn't that the reason you married me? To have your own life rather than one he chose for you?"

She spun away from him, fighting the tears that suddenly threatened. "I can't believe I've been writing to him, thinking that after a while he'd forgive me for leaving home like that. And all this time he'd been—" She stopped because her voice threatened to break. She took a deep breath, then another, and another, until she felt able to express herself in a calm, rational manner. Then she turned around and faced him.

"All right, Bobby. At least we understand each other now. I suppose you did what you felt was best, but from now on, I will make all my own decisions. I don't need you in my life, okay? I'm here now. I don't mind staying for a few more weeks, and then I'm out of here. I'll see my lawyer and see what he suggests. I may have to file for a divorce rather than an annulment. But I will see that any ties between us are severed once and for all.''

He gave her an amused look. ''You just do that, sugar. Oh, and by the way, you will let my friends, including Frankie, of course, know when I'm no longer married to you, won't you? It's the least you can do for me, since you were so eager to let her know we're married.''

If he weren't already lying there helpless on the couch, she would have attacked him right there. How dare he patronize her! How dare he make fun of her! Who did he think he was, anyway?

She stormed out of the room before she lost control and swung at him, injuries and all. Never in all her life had she been so angry. What was it about Bobby Metcalf that so infuriated her? She'd never met another person who could affect her so strongly.

She could hardly wait to get away from him. She could hardly wait until she never had to lay eyes on him again.

Darn him, anyway! He knew exactly who he was.

Her husband.

Chapter Ten

Casey had been at the ranch six weeks before the celebrated Castillo dinner dance took place. The plans for the party had been held in abeyance while an unusual weather pattern developed over the area. For several weeks the area had been buffeted by a mixture of turbulent winds and hard-driving rain, soaking the area. Since the size of the party meant it would have to be held outdoors, the Castillos had notified prospective guests of the delay.

Now it was Saturday night and Casey was driving her car, following Bobby's directions without comment. She turned off the county road onto the private drive leading to the Castillo Ranch. There had been no conversation between them since leaving the ranch. For that matter, there had been very little conversation between them for the past six weeks.

What, after all, did they have to say to each other?

Bobby's physical condition had improved a great deal during these past weeks. He'd had the cast removed a few days ago, although he kept a cane with him to ease the strain on the weaker leg.

Casey had told Bobby yesterday that she would be returning to her apartment on Monday, now that he was out of the cast. It was one of the few times she had seen him, as he spent increasing amounts of time working out on the ranch. If she'd expected him to make some sort of protest, or to even comment, she would have been disappointed.

He'd just nodded and gone in to shower before eating supper.

Most mornings Bobby had already eaten and left the house by the time she woke up. Casey wondered why she'd stayed this long, since it was obvious he didn't need her help.

However, she felt committed to help him as she'd agreed to do. Therefore, she'd continued to have hot meals waiting for him each day. He was politely complimentary.

When Bobby asked if she wanted to go to the Castillo party she'd informed him that she wouldn't miss it for the world. In truth, she was curious to learn more about Bobby's neighbors, and since Frankie hadn't been over again, she figured this was the only way she would be able to satisfy her nosiness.

In preparation for the event she had gone into the nearest large town and shopped, looking for the perfect outfit to wear to such a gathering. Bobby had never seen her dressed up. Not that it mattered to her, of course, but she wanted to let the neighbors know that she wasn't anybody's baby sister.

Despite his silence as he'd appraised her when she walked out of her room tonight, she felt that she had succeeded.

The dress was bronze colored and brought out that shade in her hair as well as her eyes. It wasn't revealing, nor did it cling, but she felt very feminine in it.

What she had forgotten to consider was that she had never seen Bobby in anything other than jeans. Tonight he wore a black, Western-cut suit that flared over his boots. He'd had his hair trimmed yesterday so that it clung to the shape of his head. At the new, shorter length, his hair had a tendency to curl along the nape of his neck and around his ears.

He had never looked more attractive to her.

She felt certain that Frankie would be all over him once he walked into the party. Not that it mattered to Casey, of course.

Tonight would be a celebration of his return to full health and for her life to return to normal.

She couldn't be happier.

Or more relieved.

She followed the winding road through the hills for what seemed to be miles. Other cars had turned onto the road behind her, she deduced from the headlights in her rearview mirror.

"Must be quite a gathering," she said half under her breath.

"Yeah. It's an annual thing I understand they've been doing for years. I guess people really look forward to it."

"Did you go last year?"

"Yeah."

"What was it like?"

"Good food, great band, lots of wine, women and song."

"Ah."

Maybe she should have offered to leave before the

party. Since he hadn't suggested it, then neither had she. Besides, she wasn't certain her curiosity would have allowed it.

She could hear the music before a bend in the road revealed the sprawling house and surrounding lawns. Having grown up with a wealthy parent, Casey wasn't easily impressed, but the Castillo place made the home where she'd grown up look like a tract home.

For one thing, her father had built his home. She had a hunch that the Castillo family had had this place in the family for several generations. No doubt it had been built when labor was cheap and materials plentiful.

The white adobe walls gleamed in the light of hundreds of yard lights spread across the area. A tennis court had been converted into a dance floor and the kidney-shaped swimming pool was covered with floating candles flickering in the night and reflected by the gleaming water.

It looked as though the entire population of the county, maybe of West Texas, had turned out in their finest.

"Wow," she murmured, as parking attendants signaled to her where she should park.

She heard Bobby's chuckle. "At least 'wow,'" he agreed.

"Who are the Castillos, anyway? I've never heard the name."

"I hadn't, either, until after I moved here. They like to keep a low profile in the state. I understand Alfonso has a great deal of land, cattle, oil and gas interests, as well as investing wisely in various enterprises."

"Is Frankie his only child?"

"Oh, no. They have a large family, I understand, although I haven't met all of them."

Bobby came around the car and opened her door before she could get out. "You don't have to do that. Remember your leg."

"I'm not going to forget it, believe me. Exercise is good for it unless I overdo. I'm tired of playing the invalid, Casey. I've never been good in the role."

"Really? I would never have noticed."

His white grin flashed in the shadowy darkness. He grabbed her hand, saying, "C'mon, brat. Let's go party."

He sounded happier than she'd seen him in a while. She wasn't sure why the thought depressed her. If seeing Frankie again made him happy, there was no reason for her to be bothered by that. She wanted to know that Bobby was happy.

"Did I mention how nice you look tonight?" he asked, still holding her hand in his as they walked toward the lights, music and laughter of several hundred people.

"No, you didn't."

"Is the dress new?"

"Uh-huh. I don't have reason to dress up much."

"Me, neither."

"Is the suit new?"

He laughed. "Nope. I've had it for some time, but don't have much occasion to wear it."

"You look very handsome tonight, Bobby," she said, fighting the sudden lump in her throat.

He gave her hand a quick squeeze and said, "Thanks."

As soon as Casey saw Frankie, her heart sank. The woman looked drop-dead gorgeous in a filmy scarlet gown that lovingly wrapped around her body, showing off cleavage, her small waist and her curving hips. She stood beside an older man who Casey suspected was her father.

She was right. As Casey and Bobby approached the couple who were greeting the newest arrivals, she heard Frankie say, "There you are. Dad, here comes Bobby and Casey Metcalf." She took a step toward them and in a scolding voice, said, "I began to think you weren't coming!"

Bobby smiled. "Sorry, but I had a little problem with some stubborn machinery that I had to repair before I could stop work for the day." He glanced at Casey and said, "This is Alfonso Castillo, Francesca's father."

"I'm very pleased to meet you, Casey," Alfonso said, taking her hand in his. "Francesca told me that you live here now. How do you like it here in West Texas?"

"Oh, I was born near Cielo, so I'm familiar with the country."

"She's Graham Carmichael's daughter," Bobby added quietly.

"Well, then you certainly know what ranching is all about," Alfonso said, smiling. "How is your father?"

"Fine, as far as I know."

Frankie was busy studying Bobby. "You're looking fit, Bobby," she said in the lull of the conversation. "When did you get out of the cast?"

"Earlier this week. I'm still using the cane since my leg is a little weak."

She turned to Casey. "Let me take you around and introduce you to everyone." She glanced at Bobby from beneath her thick, black lashes and said, "I think you'll be able to find the bar just fine, won't you?"

Casey found Bobby's grin devastatingly attractive and wondered if her knees were the only ones that went weak when he flashed it. "Oh, yeah." He glanced at Alfonso. "May I bring you something, since it doesn't look as though your role of greeter is going to let up anytime soon?"

"Sounds good." He mentioned a mixed drink, and Bobby moved away from them and was soon lost to Casey's view.

"That dress adds a few years, I have to admit," Frankie said as they walked around the swimming pool. "I swear when I first saw you I thought you were barely sixteen."

"I know. I've always looked young for my age."

"Bobby must have been able to see through that disguise. How long have you been married?"

"A little over four years."

"Then you must be much older than I suspected."

"Not really. I was barely eighteen."

"I hope you didn't take offense at my earlier remark, honey. I didn't mean anything by it. And I have a hunch that, with those eyes of yours, Bobby didn't have any trouble recognizing your feminine qualities." She gave Casey a brief, sideways glance. "I meant what I said to you, though. It's not good to leave a man on his own for long periods of time. I learned that lesson the hard way. Just a friendly warning."

Casey was taking in all the activity around her. Thankfully spotting the long buffet table, she changed the subject by saying, "The food looks wonderful. Did your family prepare it?"

"Some. The caterers did most of it. Are you hungry?"

Casey grinned. "Starving. I think I skipped lunch today."

"Then we can take care of that right now."

It was more than an hour later before Casey had an opportunity to look around for Bobby. She'd met so many people that names and faces were whirling around in her head.

She'd spent the evening sipping on one glass of wine. So far, the glass was still more than half-full.

When she spotted Bobby she noticed that he was laughing and talking with a group of people gathered around a large round table. Numerous bottles of beer were on the table, full and empty. She hadn't seen him that relaxed and amiable since the summer they'd met. Obviously the beer had helped.

She hesitantly started toward the table, wondering if she should intrude. As soon as Bobby saw her he waved her over. "C'mon over here, Casey, and see who's here."

Once she got close enough she recognized several familiar faces from the rodeo circuit. Several jumped up and boisterously greeted her with hugs and smacking kisses. She couldn't help laughing at their enthusiasm.

It was Bobby who surprised her by pulling her down across his thighs and wrapping his arm firmly around his waist. "I told you she was here, somewhere," he said, grinning. He nuzzled her ear and said, "They accused me of hiding you away so nobody could find you. Reckon that would work?"

"Something tells me you haven't eaten yet, have you?"

"Nope."

She grinned and shook her head. "You're going to pay for this in the morning, you know."

"So what? You're no longer my nurse. Besides, didn't you say you were leaving?"

"Oh, is that what this is? An early celebration of my departure?"

He laughed. "Prickly, aren't you?"

One of the men across the table said, "I've been giving Bobby here a bad time. Y'all have been married for years, and he says there's not a single bambino to be seen around the place. The ol' boy is obviously not doing his job."

The rest of them laughed uproariously at his crude attempt at humor.

"I told them you've been away getting educated."

"Can't say as I blame her," another one said. "Who'd want to put up with your ugly mug all the time."

"Why don't you come over to the buffet with me," she said, uncomfortable with the conversation and the intimacy of sitting on his lap.

"Good idea."

She stood and waited while he said his goodbyes all around, then draped his arm across her shoulders. "Where's your cane?" she asked.

"Don't know. I probably don't need it."

"Uh-huh." Actually she didn't mind having his arm around her. It was the way he used to walk around the rodeo grounds with her, making it clear who she was with. He hadn't been this close to her in weeks.

"Are you having fun?" he asked, waving to various people who spoke to him.

"Actually, I am. I was surprised to see a few faces I recognized. They talked to me as though they thought my dad and I were still in touch. None of them seemed to think it strange that I had married you, or at least they were too polite to bring up Steve's name."

"I wouldn't have been surprised to see him here tonight. He was here last year."

She stopped walking, causing him to get overbalanced for a moment. He gripped her more tightly. "How about giving a warning when you decide to brake, okay?"

She turned and looked at him. "Why didn't you mention that Steve might be here before now?"

He shrugged. "'Cause I didn't think about it until now. Why?"

"You didn't think I'd want to know?"

"Look, Casey. There are all kinds of people in the world, even spurned fiancés. Not everybody cares whether or not they run into them occasionally."

"Obviously you don't. Your former fiancée is still your best friend!"

"Are we fighting again?"

"Oh, c'mon. Let's get some food inside you to help soak up the beer."

"Hey, now. I'm not drunk."

"I never said you were."

"Besides, I'm not the one driving."

"I know."

"I don't get out much, you know. This is the first time I've been anywhere since their party last year. Why are you making something of this?"

"I'm not, Bobby. Look at all this food. Doesn't it smell great?"

"Mmm-hmm. Have you eaten?"

"When we first got here, but I could certainly sample some more of this. Here's a plate. Let's graze."

Bobby watched her as Casey enthusiastically placed several tidbits of food on her plate, then slowly followed her lead. Damn, but she was beautiful tonight. Seeing her all dressed up for the first time had taken his breath away.

And she was leaving on Monday.

This time he knew that the separation would be final. After all, there was no reason for them to see each other again. No reason at all.

Even if he was too broke to be able to support a wife anytime soon, he knew it was more than a lack of money that had ended his dreams where Casey was concerned. Hell, they couldn't be in the same room together for more than five minutes without fighting.

Arguing with her didn't mean anything to him, of course. It was a way of life as far as he was concerned. In fact, he rather enjoyed watching her get all steamed up over the silliest things.

Okay, so maybe he'd had a few beers tonight. It was a party, wasn't it? Time to kick back and enjoy…and for a few hours try to forget that she was leaving.

She led the way over to a small table and he sat down across from her.

They ate in silence. She'd been right, the food was delicious and he'd been hungry. He knew she wasn't comfortable with the rough crowd he used to run with. He didn't see much of them anymore since they no longer had rodeoing in common. It was a young man's sport. He'd discovered that he didn't miss it as much as he'd thought he would.

Not like he knew he would miss Casey.

He didn't want to think about that. Monday would come soon enough.

"Wanna dance?" he asked once they finished their meal.

The band had been playing slow songs that didn't

take much footwork. He thought he could handle it. And it would be nice to have her in his arms for a little while.

She'd been watching the dancers and looked around at him in surprise. "Are you sure you can?"

"Hell, no. I've never been much on a dance floor. But I'm willing to try it if you are."

"I meant because of your leg."

"Don't worry. I won't try any fancy steps. Mama never raised a dancin' fool."

She laughed, her eyes sparkling in the lights scattered around them. "We've never danced together. Let's try it."

There were lots of things they hadn't done together, but Bobby didn't want to think about any of them. Not now.

Once on the dance floor he pulled her into his arms and held her close, moving in time with the music. By necessity, she draped both arms around his shoulders. He loved the way they fit together.

As though their bodies knew how well they belonged together.

One song moved into another, and another. Bobby was memorizing everything about her for those future nights when he was going to be all alone—the freshly washed scent of her hair, the curve of her cheek, the way she danced on tiptoe, her body pressing against him, arousing him.

He brushed his mouth against hers, and she closed her eyes and sighed as though she had been waiting for that. He did it again, pausing to gently probe her lips.

Her lips parted ever so slightly and he tightened his hold around her.

She made no effort to pull away from him.

When he finally lifted his head, he knew he was in

serious trouble. His body ached with tension, he wanted her so badly.

"Do you have any idea how much I want to make love to you?" he whispered.

Her mouth glistened from their recent kiss. She opened her eyes and looked up at him. "Really?" Her eyes seemed to sparkle as though filled with diamonds.

"Oh, yeah."

"Now?"

"Anytime, anywhere, you name it."

"Do you want to go home?"

"Yes, ma'am, I sure do."

"The party will go on for hours."

"We could have our own party...just the two of us."

"I'd like that," he heard her whisper, and he was certain his heart was going to stop beating right then and there.

Without another word he took her hand and led her off the dance floor, glad of the shadows and the cut of his suit that helped to conceal his condition. He paused just long enough to tell Alfonso they were leaving. If their host thought it was because of his injuries, Bobby saw no reason to correct him.

This time he got into the driver's side of the car, and drove home in record time. He pulled up in front of the house and got out.

"Aren't you going to put the car up?"

"I'll do it in the morning," he growled, and saw her smile an instant before he helped her out of the car and directly into his arms.

Chapter Eleven

Bobby couldn't remember how they got inside the house, but somehow they were in his bedroom. He had left the hall light on before going out. Now it was the only light they had in his room, but that was just fine with him. He could see Casey, and that was all that mattered to him.

He noticed that his hands were trembling as he turned her so that her back was to him. He found the zipper in the back of her dress and lowered it, and the material parted revealing the beautiful, satiny curve of her bare back.

She hadn't been wearing a bra. He closed his eyes at the sudden realization, knowing that if he'd discovered that piece of information any earlier, he wouldn't have been able to hang on to his control this long. Hell, they might not have made it out the front door.

He slid the dress off her shoulders and watched as it silently settled around her feet.

He turned her around—slowly and with great care—

feeling as though this was all of his Christmases rolled up in one and he'd received the present he'd wanted for years.

And now it was here before him, waiting for him to enjoy, explore and learn.

She was backlit by the hall light shining through the door, which caressed her sides and left the front of her in shadows. She waited quietly, making no effort to hide herself from his eyes.

Her skin glowed in the soft light, her body completely exposed to him except for tiny briefs that rode high on her hips, then dipped to a deep vee in front.

Dear Lord, but she was the most beautiful, exciting, delectable woman he'd ever known. He'd been dreaming about her for years, waiting for her to grow up, waiting for her to want him.

Only then did he notice that her hands were busy, too—loosening his string tie, opening the buttons of his shirt, pushing at his jacket, reaching for his chest where her fingers suddenly found him, causing his skin to ripple with chills.

She gave a shaky laugh and said, "It's not fair. You have on more clothes than I do—did." She sounded breathless...and excited.

He peeled out of his jacket and shirt, then paused, shaking his head ruefully. "Sugar, there's just no easy way to get out of these damned boots."

She gave him a little push, overbalancing him so that he fell across the bed with a slight bounce. Before he understood what she was doing she turned and straddled one of his legs. "C'mon," she said with a chuckle, "I'll help." She tugged on his boot until it came off, then straddled his other leg. She glanced over her shoulder.

"Help me," she said, sounding a little breathless from the exertion.

He knew what she wanted, and placed his stocking-clad foot against her bottom, his toes curling against the muscled posterior as she freed his other foot. Pivoting, she leaned over and started working his belt buckle, her palms and knuckles inadvertently brushing against his very rigid length.

He groaned and laughingly brushed her hands away. "You'd better let me do that, sugar, or this show will be over before it gets started."

She stepped back from him, and he wasted no time in loosening the belt and unfastening his trousers. He slid them off his hips, and she pulled from the hems of the pant legs, tossing them aside before crawling onto the bed beside him.

He was still sideways on the bed, but somehow none of that mattered at the moment. He seemed to have caught on fire, fueled by her urgency as well as his. All he knew at that moment was he wanted her more than he'd wanted anything or anyone in his life.

She was shaking, he noticed, and he paused for a moment. "Are you cold?"

"Uh-uh. A little nervous, maybe."

Of course she would be. She'd told him during that summer they were together about the fights she'd had with Steve when she hadn't wanted to make love with him, so he'd known that she'd never been with a man before. At the time, he'd tried to convince himself that her virginal condition didn't have anything to do with him. That someday her husband, her real husband, would be the one to show her what this part of married life was like.

Now, he was the one who would be showing her,

who would be loving her, who hopefully could make the experience a pleasurable one.

Or he would die trying.

He ran his hand lightly along her body, getting her used to his touch, much as he did when soothing one of his horses. She stiffened at first, catching her breath, and he waited for her to relax before moving his hand once again. There was no rush, he kept reminding himself, feeling her startled response when he brushed across her breasts with the back of his fingers.

He took his time, fighting his own sense of urgency, his own need for completion, his own rigid pain. He wanted her to be with him every step of the way.

He knew he was succeeding in his efforts when she reached over and touched him, her hand lingering at his waist before she ran a finger beneath the waistband of his briefs. She was responding to him, thank God, shyly following his lead.

She reached up and pushed her hand through his hair, her little finger circling the inside of his ear before she pulled his head closer and pressed her lips against his.

She made a soft sound of satisfaction when he took over the kiss, feverishly taking possession.

He wanted to go slow, to take his time, but Casey seemed to have something else in mind, and he was soon fighting for control of his own body, which threatened to betray his need at any moment. Without being fully conscious of when and how it happened, Bobby realized he was now between her legs, and she was holding him so tightly he could scarcely get his breath.

She might never have done this before, but she sure knew what she wanted, and she wanted it now.

Who was he to discourage a lady's wishes?

He tried to be careful but he knew he hurt her despite

everything he could do. Not that he'd had much experience with women, especially innocent ones. He paused, not knowing what to say or do, wondering if he should pull away, but her grip only tightened. Instinct took over. He began to move, and she shifted slightly in an effort to accommodate him, her soft sigh of pleasure reassuring him.

His release rushed everything, coming much too soon when he wanted to savor this moment. However, there were just some times when the mind couldn't control the body's needs.

Bobby cried out, tears filling his eyes. He could no longer contain all the different feelings racing inside of him. He tried to get his breath as well as a grip on his emotions, leaning on his arms so that his weight didn't crush her.

There was only the sound of their heavy breathing in the room for a while, until he could find the breath to speak.

"I'm sorry it wasn't better for you," he whispered gruffly.

"Don't apologize," she whispered back before she began to place kisses on his chin, his neck, and down across his chest.

He sighed and relaxed one arm so that he rolled onto the bed, still holding her close with his other arm. "Oh, Casey," was all he could say before he seemed to lose consciousness. His last awareness was holding her in his arms.

He didn't know how long he'd been asleep, but when he next opened his eyes it was still dark and he had a raging thirst. He leaned up on his elbow and looked around.

They were still lying on top of the bedclothes, across

the bed, and Casey was curled against his side. With the way he'd been feeling earlier, they'd been damned lucky to make it to the bedroom!

Shaking his head at his own behavior, he sat up, then slipped off the bed and walked quietly into the bathroom. When he came back, he reached into the hall and turned off the light, leaving the room in darkness. He felt his way back to the bed and turned the covers back before slipping his arms beneath Casey and picking her up.

"Where are you taking me?" she murmured, still more asleep than awake.

"To bed, sugar. I'm just taking you to bed."

He placed her beneath the sheet and slid in beside her. She reached for him and he made no effort to discourage her.

They were both more than half asleep, giving their lovemaking this time a dreamlike quality. Because he was so nearly asleep, Bobby found it perfectly natural to murmur to her, encouraging her to explore him as he stroked her receptive body. He kissed and caressed her, careful to lead her to that place where she could find her own intense release at last, then holding her as she trembled in his arms.

And much like a dream, they drifted into a deeper slumber after their lovemaking, wrapped in each other's arms.

The sound of heavy rain falling woke Casey several hours later, and she thought about the party and wondered if everyone there had gotten away before the rain started. Then she opened her eyes and saw that it was daylight, although still a dark day. She squinted at the clock and was surprised to see that it was after ten o'clock.

She hadn't slept that late in years.

Her eyelids fluttered closed while she listened to the sound of the rain on the tin roof. It was almost a musical sound, one she had enjoyed during these past few weeks of rain. At least the hills would be beautifully green this summer.

She was dozing back to sleep when she remembered where she was. How could she have possibly forgotten? She raised her head and looked at the man who sprawled beside her in the bed, his head half buried under his pillow.

How many times had she seen him like that their first summer together, while they shared those cheap little motel rooms? Wow! If she'd only known then what she was missing by not having an intimate relationship with him!

Last night had been magical, from the time he'd taken her out on the dance floor until he'd shown her what she had been missing with him all these years. My, oh, my, but he was something.

And she loved him.

The thought no longer surprised her. She'd probably loved him for years and had been too dumb to know it. The big question now was, what was she going to do about it? She loved him, and she wanted to stay married to him, but she wasn't ready to give up her lifelong dream of becoming a vet.

Hadn't Frankie warned her that she shouldn't leave him if she wanted their marriage to last? What was it she wanted the most? And why couldn't she have both?

Giving in to the temptation presented to her, Casey ran her hand across the broad expanse of his muscled, tanned back. He was one fine specimen of a virile male animal, that was certain.

Her mind and body tingled with memories of all that they had done together the night before. Parts of her body were protesting slightly, but she ignored them in her desire to once again experience all that she had learned during the past few hours.

With that in mind she inched closer to him and, instead of using her fingertips, she pressed a row of kisses across his shoulders and down his spine, loving the slight indentation where the muscles connected along the length of him.

Sometime during that careful exploration of every inch of his back he turned over, his eyes still closed, but with a decided lift to the corners of his mouth.

She didn't mind exploring on this side of him, either.

By the time she reached his pelvic area he pulled her over him, placing her legs on either side of him, and showed her just how easily they fit together in that position as well.

She could now control their coming together, and she experimented with the timing and rhythm, aware that he was watching her from beneath his thick lashes. Neither one of them had said a word since waking up that morning.

Sometimes words weren't really necessary to communicate, at all.

Chapter Twelve

Casey was in the kitchen sometime mid-afternoon when she heard Bobby stirring in the back of the house. When she'd slipped out of bed he had been sound asleep once again. Instead of awakening him, she had taken a shower in the hall bathroom, dressed and headed to the kitchen.

She was starved and she had a hunch that Bobby would be, as well. Now the coffee was ready and she had several strips of bacon done and was preparing eggs and toast.

Trying to be casual, she merely glanced at him when Bobby came into the kitchen. It was difficult not to react to the sight of him in snug jeans that were zipped but unbuttoned at the top, a shirt that hung open, revealing the taut muscles of his chest and abdomen, and his feet bare. His hair was still damp from his shower, although he'd taken time to comb it back from his face.

So she busied herself with the food without comment.

"Coffee smells good," he rumbled in a sleepy voice, reaching for a mug and filling it with the fresh brew.

"Breakfast will be ready shortly."

"Breakfast? At—" he paused and glanced at the kitchen clock "—four o'clock in the afternoon?"

"It's still the first meal of the day," she replied in a neutral voice, not looking at him.

When he didn't say anything more, she risked another glance at him. He was now seated at the table, sipping at his coffee and watching her.

She couldn't figure out what there was to look at that was so interesting. She wore what she generally wore— her jeans, a shirt and loafers. She'd pulled her hair back into a ponytail rather than attempt a more elaborate hairdo.

"You feelin' all right?" he asked after a lengthy silence had spread between them.

She placed a full plate of steaming food in front of him, refilled his cup and sat down across from him with her similarly filled plate.

How could she answer that? Physically, she was more than a little tender in several vulnerable spots. Emotionally, she was very confused. Mentally, her brain seemed to have vacated its usual place in her head so that she was running on autopilot.

She opted for politeness. "Fine. And you?"

He made a face, shook his head, and began to eat as though he were starving. Bobby waited until his plate was polished clean and he was sipping on yet another cup of coffee before speaking again.

"You mad at me?"

Casey jumped up and began to clear the dishes, busying herself with filling the wash pan with water and soap, wiping down the table and countertops, doing anything that kept her from looking at him.

"Why should I be mad?" she finally asked.

He sighed a rather gusty sigh. "For starters, I drank more than I'm used to last night."

"There's nothing criminal about that. Most people do at a party."

"Casey?"

"Mmm?"

"Stop trying to scrub the design off the countertop and look at me."

She forced herself to turn, leaned against the very clean counters, folded her arms and stared at him, striving to look calm and casual.

"Yes?"

"I'd hate to think that I might have taken advantage of you last night."

Now that she was really looking at him, she realized that he was as uncomfortable with her as she was with him. Was he regretting what had happened between them? Was he sorry? Was he saying that the only reason they had made love was because he'd been drinking and she was available?

She cleared her throat. "I'm an adult, Bobby, capable of making my own decisions. I didn't drink too much last night and if you have any recollection of what happened, you'll recall that I was an active participant."

"Well, hell, Casey, I didn't have so much beer that my memory's gone!"

"It wouldn't be the first time your memory was an issue between us."

He muttered an unprintable obscenity beneath his breath.

"Are you still leaving in the morning?" he asked after another lengthy silence.

She froze. What was he really asking? Did he expect her to give up all of her plans and dreams, now that she had become his wife in fact as well as in name?

"I need to get ready for classes," she said in a careful voice, unsure of what to say. "They'll be starting soon."

He got up, drained his cup of the remaining liquid, then walked over and washed it in the soapy water. After carefully rinsing it, he put it in the drain. Without saying anything more, he walked out of the kitchen and down the hall.

Well, she thought defensively, what had he expected her to say? That she loved him, that she wanted to stay married to him, that she would be content to live here with him for the rest of her life?

Actually, the thought of staying here for the next fifty years held an enormous appeal to her. Sleeping next to Bobby night after night, waking up next to him each and every morning would be a joy to her.

And yet—

She couldn't remember a time when she hadn't wanted to be a veterinarian. Loving Bobby didn't change any of that.

Frankie's words kept echoing in her head. If she went back to school after all they had shared, Bobby would be alone...and Frankie was very available, obviously attracted to him, and was no doubt everything he could possibly want and need.

Casey reminded herself that Bobby had never told her he loved her, not even during their many hours of love-making. She wasn't totally naive. She knew that a man didn't have to love a woman in order to make love to her. For all she knew, he had made love to Frankie dozens of times—hundreds of times—thousands—Okay, maybe dozens of times.

The more she thought about it, the angrier she got. What did he want from her, anyway?

She heard him coming down the hall again, the echo of his boot heels tracking his progress. When he appeared in the doorway this time, he was completely dressed with his shirttail tucked in. She wanted to accuse him of cheating on her for the past four years, even though she knew the accusation was absolutely ridiculous. They hadn't had the kind of relationship where there had been any kind of commitment between them.

It was just that everything had changed now. Hadn't it? Did their making love change anything at all between them? She had already realized that they would need to sever their legal ties with a divorce, so nothing that happened last night…or this morning…had jeopardized the future.

"Bobby?"

He paused, holding the screen door open. She absently noted that sometime during the day the rain had stopped, but it looked cloudy and threatening outside as though the rain could start up again any minute.

"What?" He sounded irritated at the interruption.

"What do you want from me?" she asked quietly.

She watched him struggle with some kind of emotion. He seemed to be sorting through words, or possibly feelings. After knowing him as long as she had, she knew that Bobby Metcalf wasn't the most articulate man in the world. He was a man of action, not words.

He adjusted his hat, pulling it down low over his eyes before he answered her, his voice raspy. "Not a damned thing, Casey. I've already been paid well for all my services.''

He let the screen door slam behind him.

She felt as though he had struck her.

For the rest of the afternoon Casey cleaned the small house until every inch of it was gleaming with soap and polish. Then she went to her room and carefully packed all of her belongings.

She wished she could cry. Her throat ached with unshed tears, but the pain went too deep. What had she wanted him to say, after all? They had made a silly bargain, and he had lived up to the letter and spirit of that bargain. What more could she have possibly expected?

Sometime around dusk she heard his truck start up. She peeked out the window and saw the newer truck he'd bought to replace the wrecked one pull out of the driveway. She didn't want to speculate on where he was going. Besides, she was pretty sure she already knew.

Casey didn't sleep well that night. She kept waking up, listening to see if Bobby had come back. Twice she tiptoed down the hall to see if he had come in while she was asleep, but his bed was still freshly made and untouched.

By the time the sky lightened she knew he wouldn't be back. At least, not as long as she was there. It didn't take long for her to load the car, especially since it still sat in front of the house where they had left it Saturday night.

She had been on a giant emotional roller coaster since then—lifted higher than she'd ever been, then hitting bottom with a painful crash.

She toyed with leaving him a note, then decided not to bother. What, after all, could she say? Thanks for teaching her so much about herself? Thanks for allowing her time to grow up and fall in love with him? Or how about, "Don't worry, the divorce papers will be in the mail shortly."

She drove out of the ranch yard without seeing either Slim or Pablo. She didn't want to go into the barn. She didn't want to see the foal one more time.

Casey had thought that leaving her home and father was the hardest thing she'd ever had to do, but somehow it paled in comparison to what was happening to her now.

This time she was leaving her heart.

Chapter Thirteen

Bobby prayed that his head would fall off his shoulders, just to give a slight easing of the throbbing pain that filled it. He lay there wondering if he'd been in yet another accident, or maybe been thrown off a bull. He hoped to be able to come up with any explanation that would somehow cause the pain to become manageable, but so far, nothing was working.

He squinted in an effort to recognize his surroundings without letting too much light fracture his brain. Unfortunately that didn't help. He had no idea where he was.

His stomach roiled. He was afraid he was going to throw up, so he pulled himself into a sitting position, carefully holding his head while he propped his elbows on his thighs...his denim clad thighs.

What the hell? What was he doing in bed fully dressed, down to his boots?

Bits and pieces of the previous evening flitted across his brain. He remembered driving to town. He remembered going into the local hangout and ordering straight shots of bourbon. Sometime during the evening he'd switched to boilermakers—chasing the shots with beer.

He seemed to recall getting into a fight with some-body. Maybe two somebodies. Things were sort of blurred after that.

Bobby managed to stand and feel his way into a bath-room. Fumbling with his boots, he eventually stripped off his clothes and stood beneath a shower of hard-driving water, bracing himself against the shower wall with his hands, letting the water hit him in punishment for all his sins.

Stupid jerk. What had he expected her to do? Forget about going back to school? Suddenly fall in love with him? Forget she was Graham Carmichael's daughter and be willing to settle for somebody like him?

Wouldn't she be impressed with him this morning, if she could see the shape he was in. At least he'd had sense enough to stumble to the motel next to the bar and get a room. He'd been in no shape to drive last night. He wasn't certain he could drive now, as far as that went.

The water was running cool by the time he shut it off. He groped for a towel and absently patted most of the moisture from his face and body before realizing that his hair was still dripping rivulets of water down his face as fast as he wiped them away.

Eventually he found his way back to the bed and carefully eased his poor, battered body down on it. He wasn't in any hurry to go anywhere. He knew she would be gone when he got back to the ranch.

It was better this way.

It was late afternoon when Bobby finally got back home. His clothes stank of beer, bourbon and cigarette smoke. The first thing he did was change clothes. The second thing he did was to wander through the house, idly noting how fresh and clean everything looked.

The bedroom she'd used was bare, of course. She'd also changed the sheets on his bed, so that he wouldn't even have her scent on his pillow.

Nothing had really changed in his life. He had his ranch. He had his life, good friends. He had his future, just not the one he'd been hoping for when he first bought the ranch.

Graham Carmichael had unwittingly done him a favor, forcing Bobby to see himself through someone else's eyes. He hadn't liked what he'd seen, so had decided to change it. Casey Carmichael had never really figured into anything but his dreams. The reality was that because of her he had stopped drinking—well, mostly, anyway—and had gotten himself a life outside of rodeoing.

She certainly hadn't wronged him in any way.

Only now he was going to have even more memories to haunt him through the years. Now he didn't have to imagine what it would be like to make love to her. Now he knew.

As a penance for his overindulgence, Bobby got up early each morning, even earlier than usual, and spent his days doing hard physical labor around the ranch. There was always something that needed fixing on a place the size of his, and never enough help or time to get it all done.

He would fall into bed each night exhausted, too tired to dream, then get up the next morning and follow the schedule he'd set himself again. Slim pointed out that he was losing weight. He guessed he was, but it didn't really matter. He adjusted his belt to a tighter notch and went on with what needed to be done.

Bobby lost track of time, so he didn't know exactly what day it was when the phone rang just as he was coming through the door. He glanced at it in surprise, since it seldom rang. He grabbed the kitchen extension.

"H'lo?"

"How's it goin', fella?" he heard Chris say. "Have you recovered?"

The first thought that flashed through Bobby's head was that Chris was referring to Casey's leaving, before he realized that Chris didn't know that. Bobby hadn't spoken to Chris since a week or so after he'd returned home from Fort Worth.

"Oh, yeah. You know me. Too stupid to shoot, too tough to kill."

"How's Casey?"

"She's uh, well, as far as I know."

"You mean she's not there?"

"I didn't need a nursemaid, Chris. She returned to College Station some time ago."

"But I thought you were going to have her stay?"

"It was a stupid idea, the more I thought about it. She still has more schooling to finish, and there's nowhere around here for her to get it."

"Couldn't she have stayed until school was ready to start?"

"She said she needed to get back."

"When was that?"

"Hell, Chris, I don't know. I didn't mark the day on my calendar, if that's what you want to know."

"Damn, Bobby, you are one stubborn son of a gun."

"What? What are you talking about? Did you expect

me to hogtie her and force her to stay here with me? Wouldn't that have been cute. She would have had my butt up in front of a judge in nothing flat.''

''Does she know you're still married?''

''She knows.''

''So what did she say?''

''She'd take care of it.''

''I see.'' Bobby could hear a slight sigh coming from the other end of the line, but he made no effort to explain anything else. Hell, there was nothing to explain.

''Maribeth suggested I call and have you two come up for a visit. The kids are finally over their colds. We thought it would be fun to get together, maybe take in a couple of movies, show your wife some big city life.''

''That's a good idea, actually, but things are a little busy for me around here these days. You know how it is.''

''Yeah, I have a hunch I do.'' Chris was quiet for a moment. ''Look, Bobby, if there's anything I can do, let me know. If you want to bend my ear for a while just say the word and I'll come down. It's been a while since we sat around the kitchen table knocking back the brews and talking.''

Bobby absently rubbed his head, thinking of the painful hangover he'd suffered a few weeks ago. The thought of going through that again held no appeal to him. ''You know I always enjoy your company, Chris. Anytime you want to come over here, either alone or with the family, you know you're welcome.''

''But you don't want to talk about your relationship with Casey, do you?''

''I don't have a relationship with Casey, Chris. You know that. Hell, you'd never even heard of her before my wreck. She's long gone out of my life. Nothing's going to change where's she's concerned.''

''I just don't want to think of you sitting there brooding by yourself, that's all.''

Bobby chuckled. ''Me? Brood? You gotta be kiddin'. I don't have time for that nonsense.''

''Will you call me if you need to talk?''

''Sure. Haven't I always?''

''No.''

They both laughed.

When Bobby hung up the phone a few minutes later, he had a lump in his throat. Thank God for friends who knew and understood you, even when you were hurting and wanted to be left alone.

Brooding. Hell. Next thing somebody would accuse him of pining away for a lost love or something.

That only happened in books.

Autumn was always slow finding Texas. Even though the calendar listed its official arrival in September, it was more like October before the summer heat released its grip on most of the state.

The heat had bothered Casey more than usual this year. The farther east in the state a person traveled, the higher the humidity. She'd just gotten used to the West Texas dry heat, that's all. But she was glad when she woke up one morning in the middle of October to discover that a fresh Texas norther, though mild, had moved through the area the night before and helped to bring cooler temperatures.

She was finally establishing her routine in school after a rocky couple of weeks. She'd managed to catch some virus during the first few days of the fall semester and had been sicker than a dog. Somehow she'd managed to drag herself to her classes—not wanting to get behind right at the beginning—and her body had sluggishly cooperated, but the strain had taken its toll.

Now she couldn't seem to get enough rest. By the time she finished her classes each day, she barely had the energy to return to the apartment, find a quick meal and fall into bed.

On weekends she tended to sleep around the clock.

She'd finally decided to go to the drugstore and get extra vitamins to rebuild her strength. She had to do something to give herself a little pep.

Whenever she'd envisioned this year, she'd always thought she would be so excited about actually beginning her veterinarian training after all the preparatory classes she'd attended. Instead, she had to force her attention back to each class, as her mind had a discouraging way of wandering when she was supposed to be taking notes.

She kept drifting off, wondering what Bobby was doing at that moment. Or she would wonder what she would be doing if she were still at the ranch. Or she would think about Frankie Castillo. And Bobby.

She would see them together, laughing and talking. She would see them in his bedroom, laughing and—

She'd jerk her wayward thoughts to the present.

And that was the problem she was having. She couldn't keep her mind in the present. It would either jump to the past or to the future, when she would be through with school. At the moment, she felt as though she were in limbo, hanging there between past and future, her life drifting along in a routine of classwork, homework, eating and sleeping.

She thought of a saying she once read: "Life was what happened while you were making plans."

Well, she thought her present life was pitifully barren. She was depressed.

There. She'd finally admitted it to herself.

When she got home that particular Thursday evening, she decided to stop feeling sorry for herself and to do something about her yucky mood. She could go to a movie, or go over to the local watering hole and visit with some of the students who hung out over there.

Or…she could call Bobby. Just to see how things were at the ranch. She didn't even have to mention Frankie. His relationship with Frankie was none of her business. None at all.

So. Maybe she'd call Bobby, then go have a drink or see a movie. The night was young, after all. Tomorrow was Friday and there were no classes on Monday.

It took her several tries before her shaking finger could carefully choose the correct sequence of numbers on her touch-tone phone. Then she let the phone ring time after time, realizing that he wasn't even home, and still reluctant to break the slight connection she had to him and to the ranch, where his phone was continuing to ring.

Then it stopped ringing and a breathless voice said, "Hello? Hello? Are you still there?"

"Bobby?" she asked, her voice cracking slightly at the end.

"Yeah. Who's this?"

"Uh, Casey."

There was a long silence after that before she heard his voice again, sounding very cautious.

"Hi, Casey."

"Hi."

She sat there twisting the telephone cord around her

fingers, waiting for him to say something more. But he didn't.

"I, uh, was just thinking about you, and was, uh, wondering how, uh, you know, how things were going at the ranch."

"You were thinking of me?" He sounded more than a little skeptical, which immediately triggered all of her defenses. Did he think she was lying, for Pete's sake?

"Is that so strange?" she demanded with more than a little belligerence ringing in her voice.

"Yeah, it is."

"I think of you quite often, as a matter of fact!"

"That's good to hear," he replied slowly, and she could almost see the half smile on his face.

She wondered if he could hear her heart pounding as its echo seemed to fill her ears.

"I guess you're really busy these days," she offered tentatively, then waited through another long pause before he cautiously responded.

"Not too much. We've managed to catch up on the things that piled up last summer when I was laid up."

"Oh. Well, that's great. Have you had any more problems with your leg?"

"It seems good as new. The insurance adjuster keeps pestering me to sign a release, stating that everything's okay now. Guess they're afraid I'm gonna sue or something."

"I was wondering..." she began, then got cold feet. "Oh, never mind. I guess I'll let you go. I just wanted to check to see how you were doing. I'm glad everything's okay."

"What were you wondering, sugar?" he asked softly, and her heart melted into a puddle right at her feet.

She knew that tone of voice. It was the one he'd used

with her when they'd made love all those weeks ago. It was a tone she'd never heard him use with anyone else.

Casey swallowed, gathering her courage. "Well, I guess I was just wondering if maybe you'd have time to come see me this weekend." She heard the words coming out of her mouth in amazement. She'd had absolutely no idea that she was going to ask him such a question until she'd verbalized it. Not giving him a chance to respond. "We aren't having classes Monday because of some holiday or teacher's something or other, or— I don't know. So I just thought that maybe—"

"Casey. Hey, sugar, are you going to let me get a word in?"

She felt her panic mount.

"Sure," she muttered, feeling like a complete, absolute, dyed-in-the-wool fool for letting him know she wanted to see him.

"I think I could manage a weekend away," he was saying in his slow drawl. "What time will you be through with your classes tomorrow?"

"Uh, tomorrow. That's Friday. Well, I— Oh! Friday. My last class is at one. I should be home around two-thirty, maybe a little later."

"Then I'll try to get there around then."

"Do you remember how to find my apartment?"

"Sugar, I've never forgotten a single, solitary thing about you." His low voice caressed her as though his hand had physically stroked across her body.

She shivered, so aroused that she huddled in the chair, her knees together.

"Well, then I guess I'll see you tomorrow sometime,'' she finally managed to say, knowing that she sounded breathless and unable to do a thing about it.

She heard his deep, rumbling chuckle, as though he knew what she was feeling and how she was reacting to him.

''Yes, you will. You can count on it,'' he said before hanging up.

Chapter Fourteen

Bobby was sitting in his truck parked in her driveway when Casey got home Friday afternoon, his hat pushed over his eyes as though he were dozing.

She pulled up beside him, her heart hammering so hard she wondered if she could be having a heart attack. She didn't know what to say to him now that he was here. Her time in class had been completely wasted as she'd worked on various things she could say to him—casual things, lighthearted things.

He'd been willing to come see her. She had no idea what he might expect from her now that he was here. For that matter, she wasn't certain what she expected of him, either.

He must have heard her car because he straightened and shoved open the door of his truck, adjusting his hat so that the brim effectively shadowed his face. His stance was wary as he watched her approach.

"Hi," she said, hoping she sounded relaxed. "Have you been waiting long?" She stopped an arm's length away, wondering if she should hug him, waiting for a sign from him that he wouldn't rebuff her.

Oh, but he looked wonderful to her. Wonderful! Then she looked a little closer and they both spoke at the same time, saying the same thing.

"You've lost weight."

She was startled by his comment, which didn't answer the question she'd asked him. She glanced down at herself and gave a tiny shrug before saying, "Not as much as you. You're even thinner than you were when you came home from the hospital."

"I've just been busy. How about you? What have you been doing to yourself?" he asked, frowning as he looked at her more closely.

He was looking more displeased by the moment. She answered him with a hint of nervousness. "Oh, I just picked up one of those bugs going around." She glanced around them, only now aware of the fact that they were still standing beside his truck.

"You look like the next strong breeze could blow you away."

The comment upset her. Maybe he'd forgotten that she'd never been very voluptuous. Maybe he was comparing her to— No, no, no. She didn't want to go there. At least he was here, now. That was the important thing.

"Have you eaten?" she asked, in an attempt to regain her composure. "From the looks of things, we could probably both benefit from regular meals."

He glanced at her apartment, as though a little nervous. "Good idea. Let's go get something." He didn't appear eager to go inside.

"There's plenty of food here, if you'd like."

He shook his head. "No need for you to go to any trouble after being busy all day."

Maybe it was just as well. They needed to talk. Perhaps it would be better to meet in neutral territory. However, she didn't want to take him to one of the student hangouts. They were generally noisy.

Bobby helped her into his truck, then backed out of the driveway. Casey tried to think of something to say now that they were together, but her mind had shut down.

"Everything all right at the ranch?" she finally asked in an effort to ease the tension that had sprung up in the cab of his truck.

"Same as ever. Too much to do and not enough time to do it in."

"Why don't you hire some more help?"

He continued to stare straight ahead. The only reaction was a slight tightening of his jaw. "Can't afford it," he muttered. He signaled a left turn in the middle of the block and pulled into the parking area of a diner.

She waited until they were seated inside and had given their orders before she said, "You have a great deal of money at your disposal, Bobby. Why do you have to be so stubborn?"

The glare she received would have withered most people, but she ignored it.

"I suppose you're referring to the money you put in my name."

"It's your money, Bobby. That was the agreement we made and you honored your part of the agreement. I don't know why you have to be so pigheaded about it."

"In the first place, I never agreed to take any of your money. I don't want it. I don't—"

"If you're about to say you don't need it, then don't waste your breath. Your working yourself to death from the looks of it. I just don't understand why you have to be so blasted hardheaded. Honestly, Bobby, you are the most impossible man I've ever—''

"I didn't marry you for that money, Casey, and I'm sick to death of hearing about it!''

"Then why did you marry me? Out of the kindness of your heart, I suppose.''

He sat back in the booth and shook his head. "We can't be together for five minutes without fighting. I don't know why the hell I took time off to come here, anyway.''

Another blow to the heart. He was good at them, that's for sure. Casey was determined not to let him get the best of her. She took a couple of calming breaths before she said, "We didn't fight much the summer we were married. Remember?''

"I remember a lot of things about that summer and I remember we had several fights.''

"Only when you thought I was being too friendly with some of your friends.''

He looked her straight in the eye. "I'm not going to apologize for that. You were like a newborn, you were so naive. I didn't dare take my eyes off you or you'd be wandering off getting into some kind of trouble.''

A memory surfaced and she grinned. "Like that first night when those guys were hanging around my car, you mean? You came to my rescue, as I recall.''

A slow smile appeared on his face. "You've always had more guts than common sense.''

She reached over and touched his hand. "I would never have made it this far without your help, Bobby. Can you possibly understand why it is so important to me that you allow me the chance to do something for you? I have plenty of money now. I've kept my living expenses down, I've got the money set aside to start my own veterinarian practice. I don't need—''

He looked away. ''I was hoping you'd take the money in my account to help set yourself up in business.''

Their food was set in front of them, and they began to eat.

''Is there anything I can say that would make you feel better about using the money for the ranch?''

He was quiet for a long while. He didn't seem to have much of an appetite and kept moving his food around on the plate without eating much. Finally, he sighed and put his fork down.

''I guess I just don't like the idea that I could be bought off. I wanted to help you without your thinking you had to pay for it.''

''It was a business arrangement, pure and simple. I don't know why you would never accept that.''

He pushed his plate back and folded his arms on the table in front of him. His gaze looked bleak. ''Oh, I was very aware of that, Casey. I guess I was just hoping that maybe someday you might change your mind, that's all. Just shows what a dumb jerk I am, right?'' He picked up his glass of iced tea and drank. After placing it carefully on the table he met her gaze once again. ''So. Guess we need to get all this cleared up once and for all. It's dragged on for too long as it is.'' He looked through the large plate-glass window at the parking lot as though fascinated by the sight. ''If I hadn't messed up so bad the last weekend you were there, we could file those annulment papers,'' he said, his eyes still trained on something outside. ''All I can say is that I'm really sorry that I took advantage of your being there like that.''

He finally turned his head and looked at her once again. "I should have known better than to think I could play the part of a knight for anybody. I guess I thought if I rescued you, you'd—"

He didn't finish the sentence.

"Is that how you saw yourself, Bobby?" she asked softly.

"Really dumb, huh?"

"It was a very loving thing to do."

He didn't say anything for a long time, just stared down at his folded arms resting on the table. When he finally raised his eyes, she was startled to see a bright sheen of tears in them.

"Yeah. That was the dumbest thing of all, falling in love with you back then."

She couldn't believe that she'd heard him right. He was talking low, after all. Maybe she had misunderstood him...and yet the expression on his face gave proof to his muttered words.

"Bobby? Are you saying that you love me?" she whispered, her voice failing her.

"Oh, yeah. Big time. It's really ironic, isn't it? I got what I deserved. Guess I should have taken the money and been thankful. Instead, I kept trying to find a way to prove myself worthy of loving you. The only thing I could think of to do was to refuse to spend your money."

"But you never said anything."

"Of course not. That wasn't part of the agreement."

Casey's perception of her life, of Bobby, and of their entire relationship, made a subtle, life-changing shift. Everything was different in so many ways that she couldn't trace them all that fast, but she knew that her life was taking another very abrupt turn.

"So all that time we were together, sharing a room, pretending to be happily married around all your friends, you really weren't acting?"

"The act came when I pretended I wasn't interested in you when all I could think about was how much I wanted you. I'd never lived with a woman before, not like that, and I wasn't used to denying myself whatever I wanted. But you were different." He chuckled, but didn't sound particularly amused. "I never took so many cold showers in my life as I did that summer. It was certainly a character-building experience."

"And you never said a word."

"You were too young, Casey, and you'd just gone through a bad time with your father. Sure, I could have played on your emotions and seduced you. You were grateful to me and I knew that. I just didn't want your gratitude. Still don't."

"Just like you didn't want me taking care of you when you were hurt."

"I had hoped to handle things a little differently between us. The timing was all off." He picked up her hand and played with her fingers without looking directly at her. "I really messed up, then. I should never have made love to you. I knew it, but did it anyway."

"Why not? You're my husband."

"Making love to you wasn't part of the deal when you offered to look after me."

And another piece of the puzzle fell into place.

"Is that why you asked me if I was mad at you the day before I left the ranch?"

He was suddenly very busy studying her fingers, the shape of her hand, measuring the length of his hand against the length of hers. So he just nodded.

"You thought you had broken the agreement by making love to me."

"Yeah," he admitted gruffly.

She shook her head in amazement. How could she have so misunderstood a situation that, examined in this new light, made so much sense.

"Are you ready to go back to the apartment?" she asked.

He looked relieved that she had stopped questioning him. "Sure," he agreed, grabbing the check and sliding out of the booth.

She watched him walk over to the cashier, reach into his back pocket for his wallet and pull out some bills. Even with his weight loss, Bobby still managed to fill out a pair of jeans just fine.

Oh, yes he did.

Neither of them said anything as he drove them back to the apartment. She waited until they got inside before she took his hand and led him into her small bedroom. He looked at her in surprise. "What is it? Have you changed something in here?"

She grinned. "Not yet. The only thing I want to change at the moment is the amount of clothes you're wearing," she said, unsnapping his shirt buttons.

He stared down at her, as though in shock. "Casey? What do you think you're doing?"

"I'm going to show you that you aren't the only one with emotions all tied in knots in this relationship. How do you think I felt when I discovered that we were still married? How do you think I felt watching Frankie kissing you and flirting for all she was worth? I know you're a man of few words, Bobby, but— Look at the time we've wasted because you wouldn't tell me how you really felt about me."

He sat down very suddenly on the side of the bed and looked at her in shock. "Are you saying—"

"I'm saying that I've probably been in love with you for years and just didn't know it...not until I walked into that hospital room and saw you lying there so pale and still." She moved closer to him, standing between his bent legs, and draped her arms around his neck. "That's when I realized that I had never forgotten you. You were always lurking somewhere in the back of my mind and I mentally compared every man I met with you."

"Oh, sugar," he said, wrapping his arms around her waist and placing his head against her breasts.

"I love you, Bobby, and I'm sorry it has taken me so long to realize it and even longer to tell you. I thought you'd understand how I felt when I made love to you."

He straightened and cupped her face in his hands. "That was when I thought I had lost you."

The kiss he gave her was so gentle it brought tears to her eyes.

Several hours later the two of them were sprawled across her rather narrow bed. The bedspread was hanging off one side, the top sheet off the other, while the pillows were scattered on the floor.

Casey was using Bobby's shoulder as a pillow, which she found more than adequate. As a matter of fact, she was lying there thinking that she never wanted to move again, even though she knew that sooner or later they would have to eat something, or shower, or rejoin the rest of the world.

But not now, thank goodness. Now she was exactly where she wanted to be.

"Are you asleep?" she asked softly, not wanting to disturb him if he'd dozed off. After all, he'd had a long drive to get there, and she'd kept him rather active since he'd arrived.

"If I am, don't wake me up," he replied, his deep voice rumbling beneath her ear.

She raised her head and looked at him. He made no effort to hide his beautifully bare body so that she had the opportunity to look him over with care.

"You haven't been eating regularly, have you?" she asked.

"Missed your cooking," he murmured with his eyes still closed.

"I tell you what. When I come home for Thanksgiving, I'll cook up a lot of extra meals to help hold you over until Christmas break. I'll be home for almost two weeks then. Between school holidays and vacations, I'll be able to fatten you up before you know it."

He opened one eye and gazed at her. "You serious?"

"As a heart attack."

"Are you going to have the time while you're still going to school?"

"The only way you'll be able to keep me away is to divorce me."

He closed his eye. "That'll never happen."

"It's a good thing you never filed those annulment papers."

He hugged her closer to him, if possible. "Glad you see it that way. I figured you'd be angry."

"Not at all. It will be much easier this way. I wouldn't have wanted to explain to our son...or maybe our daughter...that we'd rushed into marriage because he or she was on the way."

"What are you talking about? We aren't going to

have a family until after you're through with school. There's no sense in making things more difficult for you than they are already."

"Bobby, if my calculations are right, we're going to start that family in another seven months or so, education or no education."

She watched him absorb that little piece of news, knowing that sooner or later he would ask her the next question. It didn't take him long.

He shifted so that he was leaning on an elbow looking down at her. "When did you know?"

"Good question. When did I finally allow myself to put all the symptoms together and realize that whatever bug I'd picked up sure seemed to be lingering longer than usual? Oh, maybe ten or fifteen minutes ago."

He studied her for a long, solemn moment without speaking. She could understand his wariness. After all, she was the one who had called him, not the other way around.

Then he grinned, shaking his head. "And you plan to be a doctor? You'd better smarten up, sugar, or you'll have some disgruntled patients." His smile slowly faded. "I should have known better than to take that kind of chance with you. I wasn't thinking very clearly that night."

"Neither was I. And, maybe, if we'd been planning everything, we might have postponed having a baby just now. But you know something? I'm not sorry. Not at all. I can't think of anything I'd rather do than to have your baby. I can miss a semester and finish school later."

"And I'm going to see that you do, you hear me? I never want to feel that I held you back from whatever it is you want in life."

Casey threw one of her legs over him so that she straddled him, then leaned over and gave him a lingering kiss. She could have predicted the results...and she wasn't disappointed.

Rubbing her hands across his chest, she said, ''Don't worry, sugar—'' she deliberately mimicked the way he drawled the word ''—you've given me more than I ever dreamed of.''

Epilogue

"Here comes Mommy! See her, Daddy? Hi, Mommy! Here we are!" Jamie's voice was high with excitement.

Bobby was having a hard time holding him in his arms, but he didn't want to lose his son in the crowd. He, Chris and Maribeth formed a small island in the swarming sea of people that had attended the graduation ceremonies.

"Now we're going to have to call you Dr. Mommy," Chris said, greeting Casey with a big grin and an equally big hug.

"That's different, anyway," she said, laughing at his teasing while she held out her arms to her four-year-old son who fell into them. "Oomph! You're getting almost too big for me to hold, young man!" She lowered him to the ground, grasping his small hand in a firm grip.

"Especially in your delicate condition," Maribeth replied with a knowing look.

"Casey!" Bobby said in exasperation, not hiding his

shocked surprise. "You told me that there was no way you could get— I mean, you assured me that—" He stopped talking when the other three began to laugh at his sputtering response.

Casey lowered her lashes and gave him a provocative glance up and down. "Well, you know how it is, dude. There are certain times when a person will say anything at all to get what he—or in this case, she—wants." She went up on her tiptoes and gave him a lingering kiss before adding, "It's an age-old tradition, wouldn't you say?"

"Not at *our* house!" Bobby replied heatedly, causing the others to laugh even more uproariously. "I'm sure glad I'm able to help keep y'all entertained," he added irritably. "We talked about that, Casey, and we agreed—"

She interrupted him, linking her free arm with his. "I know we did. But just look at it this way. There won't be as big of an age gap between the two of them as we planned. That can only help. Besides, now that I'm out of school I can take it a little easier."

Bobby looked at her with disbelief and shook his head. "Oh, sure. Take it easy. As though you've ever understood in the least what those words mean. I had to sit on you to get you to get enough rest when you were pregnant with Jamie. Now you're going to be opening your practice, and—"

Casey looked at the other two. "Do you see what I have to put up with from morning to night? Nag, nag, nag. The man just won't shut up. But what can I do?" She kissed him again, effectively shutting him up.

"I'm hungry, Mommy," Jamie said, pulling on her hand.

"Me, too," she said, drawing away from Bobby.

"We've got reservations in Bryan, so we might as well get going." She turned to Chris and Maribeth. "I'm so glad y'all came to keep Bobby company through all of that. There is nothing more boring in the world than to sit through a long commencement ceremony."

Maribeth hugged her. "I wouldn't have missed it. I'm so proud of you for staying with it. I know it hasn't been easy for you these past few years, what with a long-distance marriage, a pregnancy and a new baby, not to mention all that studying."

"I couldn't have done it without Bobby. Too bad you can't get frequent flyer miles for road travel. He would have earned a bunch of them for all the miles he's covered between the ranch and here."

Bobby picked up Jamie once more and said, "Let's get going. Hopefully, we'll be able to find the minivan in all this crowd." He glanced over at Chris. "Did you get a room somewhere nearby?"

Chris shook his head. "No. We're going back to Agua Verde tonight and stay at the ranch. That's where the kids are. Maribeth's niece is watching them for us. How about you?"

"We'll stay at the apartment tonight. Most everything is already moved back to the ranch, but we left enough so we wouldn't have to stay in a motel. After the years I spent on the road, I don't care if I never see the inside of another one of them."

The two couples found Chris's minivan and he drove them over to the apartment where both Bobby's truck and Casey's little red car waited. "When are you going to get your wife a new car, Bobby? Hers is beginning to show its age."

"I've tried, believe me. She won't hear of it."

"That car has a great deal of sentimental value to me. It's the one we ran away in to get married."

"Oh," Chris said, "You could always have the thing bronzed. You know, like baby shoes."

"Very funny," she said when both men snickered. "I told him I don't mind getting another car. We're going to need something bigger, anyway. I just don't want to get rid of this one."

Pausing before getting out of the minivan, Bobby said, "Actually, I'd hate to see anything happen to that little car, myself."

Maribeth looked back at Casey. "Did you let your father know you were graduating?"

Casey stilled, then said, "No. It wouldn't have mattered. My father has made it very clear that he wants nothing to do with me. I've had to accept that and go on with my life."

"Maybe you should give him another chance, Casey," Maribeth said. "Every child should get to know his grandfather, right, Chris?"

He looked around at his wife. "I'll have to agree on that one. Dad is absolutely silly about our two, always has been. There was a time when I didn't care whether or not he was a part of our lives. Thank God we worked things out between us. I know the kids have benefited from having an extended family."

Casey looked at Bobby. "Since Bobby doesn't have any family left, my dad would be the only extended family we have, but it just doesn't seem to matter to me anymore. Once upon a time, my father was the most important person in my life. But it's been so long— I can't imagine that it really would matter to him."

"Well," Chris said, "We'll see you at the restaurant."

The Metcalfs transferred to Casey's car and drove behind the Cochrans to the nearby town where they had reservations for dinner. Bobby gave their name to the hostess who took them back to one of the private rooms. The table was waiting for them, and so was Graham Carmichael.

Her father.

She hadn't seen him in nine years. The years hadn't been kind to him. She remembered him as a strong, robust man filled with energy, his hair just touched with gray. Now his hair was completely white and he was a little stooped in the shoulders.

Casey froze just inside the doorway and watched as her father awkwardly stood and faced them, deliberately bracing himself for whatever reaction his presence might bring. His eyes lit up when he spotted Jamie in Bobby's arms.

Casey felt as though everybody was looking at her, waiting for her to say something...anything...but she couldn't think of anything to say.

"I hope you don't mind my being here," Graham said hesitantly. "Bobby called me a couple of weeks ago and told me that you were graduating today. He thought I might enjoy getting to know the new Dr. Metcalf and her son." He paused, as though having a little trouble with his voice. "I, uh, was touched that he contacted me."

She turned and looked at Bobby, her mind in a whirl. "You knew about this? And you didn't tell me?"

He quirked an eyebrow. "Do you think you're the only one around who keeps secrets, sugar?" He watched her intently. "So. Are we fighting?"

She shook her head, not sure whether she wanted to kick him or kiss him. How could he do this to her? How could he just expect her to forget everything that had happened, everything her father had done and not done to her and for her?

Because he was Bobby, that's why. He was always willing to give the other person the benefit of the doubt. So he'd asked her father to come. He'd given the man another chance to get to know the only family he had left.

Casey shook her head in resignation. That was Bobby, all right, and she really wouldn't want him to be any other way.

Taking a deep breath she turned to face her past.

Before she could say anything, Graham came toward her, holding out his hand. "I know I don't deserve your forgiveness, Casey, the way I treated you, the way I ignored your letters. I have no defense for my behavior and no excuse. I was wrong and I'm sorry. I've been hoping that you might be willing to forgive me and allow me to be a part of your life in whatever way you see fit." He glanced at Bobby. "I've already apologized to your husband, if that means anything to you. I'd like to think I'm big enough to admit when I'm wrong about someone. And I was wrong about you, Bobby."

Bobby smiled. "Not at all, Mr. Carmichael. I'd say you were a darn good judge of character. The way I look at it, I owe you a great deal. Without you, I would never have met Casey, never had the chance to look at myself through your eyes, never ended up with a wife I adore and a family to treasure."

Casey didn't try to hide the tears that trickled down her cheeks. Leave it to Chris to lighten the situation by saying, "Now that was downright eloquent, Bobby, old son. And here we all thought you were a man of few words. Guess anybody can change if he's got a mind to.''

Their laughter relieved the tension in the room, and eased Casey's heart as well. She reached for her dad's hand, then hugged him tightly. As soon as she could find her voice, she smiled up at him and said, ''Come on, Grandpa. There's somebody here I want you to meet.''

* * * * *

HE CAN CHANGE A DIAPER IN THREE SECONDS FLAT BUT CHANGING HIS MIND ABOUT MARRIAGE MIGHT TAKE SOME DOING! HE'S ONE OF OUR

Fabulous Fathers

July 1998
ONE MAN'S PROMISE by Diana Whitney (SR#1307)
He promised to be the best dad possible for his daughter. Yet when successful architect Richard Matthews meets C. J. Moray, he wants to make another promise—this time to a wife.

September 1998
THE COWBOY, THE BABY AND THE BRIDE-TO-BE by Cara Colter (SR#1319)
Trouble, thought Turner MacLeod when Shayla Morrison showed up at his ranch with his baby nephew in her arms. Could he take the chance of trusting his heart with this shy beauty?

November 1998
ARE YOU MY DADDY? by Leanna Wilson (SR#1331)
She hated cowboys, but Marty Thomas was willing to do anything to help her son get his memory back—even pretend sexy cowboy Joe Rawlins was his father. Problem was, Joe thought he might like this to be a permanent position.

Available at your favorite retail outlet, only from

Silhouette ROMANCE™

Take 4 bestselling love stories FREE

a FREE surprise gift!

Special Limited-time Offer

Mail to Silhouette Reader Service™

3010 Walden Avenue
P.O. Box 1867
Buffalo, N.Y. 14240-1867

YES! Please send me 4 free Silhouette Romance™ novels and my free surprise gift. Then send me 6 brand-new novels every month, which I will receive months before they appear in bookstores. Bill me at the low price of $2.90 each plus 25¢ delivery and applicable sales tax, if any.* That's the complete price and a savings of over 10% off the cover prices—quite a bargain! I understand that accepting the books and gift places me under no obligation ever to buy any books. I can always return a shipment and cancel at any time. Even if I never buy another book from Silhouette, the 4 free books and the surprise gift are mine to keep forever.

215 SEN CF2P

Name	(PLEASE PRINT)	
Address	Apt. No.	
City	State	Zip

This offer is limited to one order per household and not valid to present Silhouette Romance™ subscribers. *Terms and prices are subject to change without notice. Sales tax applicable in N.Y.

USROM-696   ©1990 Harlequin Enterprises Limited

The World's Most Eligible Bachelors are about
to be named! And Silhouette Books brings
them to you in an all-new, original series....

World's Most
Eligible Bachelors

Twelve of the sexiest, most sought-after men share
every intimate detail of their lives in twelve never-
before-published novels by the genre's top authors.

Don't miss these unforgettable stories by:

Dixie Browning

Marie Ferrarella

Jackie Merritt

Tracy Sinclair

BJ James

RACHEL
LEE   Suzanne Carey

Gina Wilkins

VICTORIA PADE

MAGGIE
SHAYNE   *Anne McAllister*

Susan Mallery

Look for one new book each month in the
World's Most Eligible Bachelors series beginning
September 1998 from Silhouette Books.

▼ *Silhouette*®

Available at your favorite retail outlet.

**Under the big sky, three unsuspecting couples
are granted their**

BEST-KEPT WISHES

In this heartwarming new miniseries by Carol Grace,
three high school friends reveal their dreams on one starry
night. Now they're all grown up and about to discover their
dearest wishes can come true—with the help of love....

GRANTED: BIG SKY GROOM   (#1277, February 1998)
Tally James longed for a ranch of her own—and wealthy rancher
Jed Whitmore owned the spread of her dreams. But would a marriage of
convenience to the groom who could fulfill all her wishes bring her
heartache—or love?

GRANTED: WILD WEST BRIDE   (#1303, June 1998)
Rugged Josh Gentry had just about given up on happily-ever-after when
beautiful Bridget McCloud showed up on his ranch, cozying up to his little boy
and kissing this single daddy till his soul caught on fire. Could this pretty city
slicker be the bride this cowboy was looking for?

And look for Suzy Fenton's story, the exciting conclusion to this irresistible
series, coming in late 1998, only from Silhouette Romance!

Available at your favorite retail outlet.

Silhouette ROMANCE™